THE
VINE
BASKET

JOSANNE LA VALLEY

HOUGHTON MIFFLIN HARCOURT
BOSTON NEW YORK

For information about permission to reproduce selections from this book,
write to Permissions, Houghton Mifflin Harcourt Publishing Company,
215 Park Avenue South, New York, New York 10003.

www.hmhco.com

The text of this book is set in Founder's Caslon.
Map art by Jennifer Thermes

The Library of Congress has cataloged the hardcover edition as follows:
La Valley, Josanne.
The vine basket / by Josanne La Valley.
p. cm.
Summary: Life has been hard for fourteen-year-old Mehrigul, a member of the
Uyghur tribal group scorned by the Chinese communist regime, so when an
American offers to buy all the baskets she can make in three weeks, Mehrigul
strives for a better future for herself and her family despite her father's
opposition.
[1. Basket making—Fiction. 2. Fathers and daughters—Fiction. 3. Farm life—
China—Fiction. 4. Ethnic relations—Fiction. 5. Uyghur (Turkic people)—
Fiction. 6. China—Fiction.] I. Title.
PZ7.V2544Vin 2013
[Fic]—dc23
2012021007

ISBN: 978-0-547-84801-3 hardcover
ISBN: 978-0-544-43939-9 paperback

Manufactured in the United States of America
DOC 10 9 8 7 6 5 4 3 2

4500549168

Uyghur is pronounced *WEEgur*.

ONE

MEHRIGUL SCANNED THE CROWDS at the market, looking for Ata. Surely by now her father had spent the yuan they'd made from the sale of a few peaches. But there was no sign of him along the dirt paths that were lined with the autumn harvest from nearby farms, the green and red peppers, the onions and potatoes piled high on donkey carts or spread out on blankets. Ata was not among those bargaining for turnips or carrots or meat cut from hanging carcasses of sheep.

He'd been gone long enough to get drunk. Wasn't that why he had brought her? Each Wednesday he left her alone with the cart for a longer and longer time.

Her gaze shifted to the mounds of honey peaches that lay unsold, the pile of willow baskets. Until her brother went away, it had been his job to come to market. Memet had insisted Mehrigul come, too, during her summer vacation. *She arranges wilted radishes so they look good enough to eat,* he'd told Ata.

She could arrange the family's goods, but she had no gift for selling. When Memet was in charge, they'd sold everything, and their legs swung happily from the edge of the empty cart as their old donkey pulled them home.

That seemed a lifetime ago. It had only been eight weeks.

"Are you all right?"

The woman selling yarn next to her had called out to her. Mehrigul was standing, gripping the edge of the cart. She forced her hands to loosen their hold and made a slow turn to face her neighbor, who sat on a crate pulling yarn into her lap, winding it into skeins.

"Would you mind watching my cart? For just a few minutes?" Mehrigul asked.

The woman waved Mehrigul away. "Take your time. Neither of us has many customers today."

Mehrigul bobbed her head. She put two peaches into a basket and walked off. A hard-boiled egg would take away the pangs of hunger, if not her troubling thoughts.

As usual, the egg woman squatted on the ground next to the seller of pots and pans. Piles of eggs and discarded shells lay on the same green ground cloth she always used. Mehrigul's classmate Hajinsa sat in front of her on a long, rolled-up rush mat she'd obviously just purchased, leaving no room for other customers who would have squatted in the accustomed manner and purchased or bartered for an egg.

Her high and mighty self sat there, her tall, slender body supple as a willow branch, her perfect red high-platform sandals and red stockings showing beneath her long blue skirt. After paying for an egg, she began peeling it, picking at the shell and carelessly dropping it bit by bit onto the ground.

The egg woman noticed Mehrigul first. Then Hajinsa glanced in her direction.

"Mehrigul, come," Hajinsa said, gesturing for her to share the seat. "Why haven't you been in school?" Rather than wait for an answer, she turned away. Blew a huff of air. "Your headscarf, tied under your chin. You try hard to look like a peasant, don't you?"

Mehrigul found her feet — no, her ugly, cheap baby strap shoes — glued to the dusty pathway.

"Better watch out," Hajinsa said, taking a bite of egg before turning around to look at Mehrigul again. "You're the kind they send to work in the factories on the coast." She hitched her shoulder. "Unless, of course, your family has lots of money to pay a fine."

Mehrigul's eyes blazed hatred at Hajinsa, but the truth in Hajinsa's words left her numb. It was already the end of October, and she hadn't been to school for even one day. She knew her name might be on the local party chief's list of girls to send away to slave in the factories of the Chinese, far from her own Uyghur people.

"Sit, Mehrigul." The voice of the egg woman broke through her stupor. "Sit next to Hajinsa. It's not often there's such a soft place to rest." She held out an egg.

Mehrigul clamped her jaws shut as she forced one offensively ugly shoe after the other over the mat and took her place.

"Have you brought something for me?" the egg seller asked.

Mehrigul handed over the peaches, basket and all, taking the egg in exchange. "My grandfather would want you to have the basket, too. Not many have sold today." Mehrigul allowed her eyes to meet those of the egg woman — kind eyes. "The basket will be good for holding throwaway eggshells."

"Thank you," the woman said, removing the peaches and setting the basket in front of Hajinsa's red shoes.

Hajinsa didn't seem to notice. She pulled money from

her pocket. Bought another egg. Again plucked off the shell in tiny pieces, letting them fall anywhere.

Mehrigul cracked her egg with a quick press of hands, peeled it, and carefully placed the shell in her grandfather's basket before taking a bite.

"So, are you coming back to school?" Hajinsa asked.

Mehrigul finished chewing her mouthful of egg. Forced herself to swallow. "Of course," she said, then twisted away for fear her face would reveal the reality she'd never admit to her classmate — that with Memet gone, there was no hope of her going to school.

As she turned from Hajinsa, she saw Ata. His back was to her, but it was unmistakably her father standing there with a group of men around a gambling table, no more than eight meters away. Mehrigul could not mistake the blue jacket she'd washed so often. The *dopa,* Ata's own brimless, four-pointed cap her mother had made for him.

Ata was throwing yuan from their morning's earnings into the pile on the caller's table.

"I must get back to my cart." Mehrigul rose, but not before the egg woman pressed another egg into her empty palm and held her hand for a moment.

Mehrigul walked past the stacks of pots and pans. At

the far side she allowed herself to steal a glance back at the gamblers. Her hands shook as she put the eggs — one half-eaten, one whole — into her pants pocket, but her mind stayed clear. She did as Memet had taught her: looked for a spy. Not Chinese; Han Chinese never came to the local market. He would be Uyghur. One of their own. Sold out to the Chinese. Paid to hang around the market dressed as a peasant, gathering information on men who might be plotting against the government. Reporting them.

Memet had been certain he was being watched. He wanted nothing to do with the Chinese Communists and their rules. He was a splittist; he wanted Uyghurs to have their own separate country where they could speak their own language and practice their own ways in freedom. Their land had once been called East Turkestan, and that was what Memet wanted again. He'd had no trouble saying bad things about the Han, only he was careful not to say anything in front of the wrong person. Ata had gotten angry when Memet talked like that, but maybe Ata was a splittist, too. Was he careful about what he said when he was drinking?

Mehrigul narrowed her eyes. There was no one behind the gamblers, only empty, shuttered stalls, a parked motorcycle. Nor was any man lingering close enough to overhear what the gambling men were saying. A few women were nearby examining kitchenware, the rows of teakettles and enamel platters and bowls spread out on the ground on the other side of the egg seller. Spies were never women, Memet had told her.

Maybe a man who drank and gambled wasn't of interest to the Chinese, Mehrigul thought as she took a long, fierce look at Ata. He was only harmful to his own family.

Ata's drinking and their poverty had already trapped Ana in her own hopeless world. Withdrawn and silent. Ashamed of being poor, she would no longer see friends. What would her mother do, Mehrigul wondered as she trudged back to the cart, if Ata were arrested and taken to a detention center?

The wool seller was in a flurry when Mehrigul returned. "A woman came. A woman came," she kept saying. Mehrigul had no idea what she meant. The piles of peaches and baskets seemed the same as when she left.

"A foreign lady," the wool seller said. "She wants to buy your basket."

"All the baskets are for sale. Three yuan," Mehrigul told her. Their neighbor had bought baskets from them before. She knew the price.

"No. No. Your special basket." The wool seller pointed

to the vine basket that hung from the crossbar on the cart, where it had been since midsummer. It was a cone-shaped basket holding a single sprig of cotton. "She's coming back," the wool seller added.

"My basket?" Mehrigul bit at her lower lip. Not believing. Wondering what she should charge. One yuan? Half a yuan? She had only twisted together some old grapevines.

Mehrigul loosened the twine that attached the basket to the crossbar and held it in front of her, for a moment remembering how her fingers had seemed to move by themselves as she and Memet sat resting near the grape arbor one summer afternoon. He kept cutting long, thin vines and she kept weaving them in and out, making a funnel about thirty centimeters high. A cornucopia, Memet said. Nothing useful like the baskets her grandfather made that could hold the wool seller's skeins of yarn or that a woman could use in her kitchen. It couldn't stand up or hold much of anything. Yet Memet had liked it and said they should use it to decorate the cart. They added the cotton to remind them of the small village where Ana had been born, a special cotton township where the women grew and spun the cotton for the men to weave. Occasionally Memet and Mehrigul stuck in a flowering squash vine for color.

Right now her cornucopia was the color of parched earth and desert sand. Mehrigul removed the cotton sprig and gave it a shake, then snapped her fingers against the cotton bolls to release more dust. She cleaned the basket with the bottom of her shirt as best she could and retied it to the crossbar.

Even as she pulled her vest down to hide the stains, she knew there was no way to conceal her soiled blouse or wrinkled pants or ugly shoes except to stand behind the cart when the lady came. But she could tie her scarf in back.

Mehrigul loosened the knot under her chin. Fluffed her hair around her face before covering it again with her scarf and tying it loosely behind her head, looking less the peasant than she really was. Maybe she'd even thank Hajinsa one day for her advice, for she'd grown careless, not bothering about how she looked. The retied scarf must have made a difference, for the wool seller caught her eye and clucked her tongue in approval.

Now Mehrigul had nothing to do but wait. She ate her eggs, bargained with the few customers who came by, and kept watching the pathways. She would have no trouble spotting a tourist; foreigners seldom, if ever, came to the

Wednesday market. The goods here were for local farmers and people who lived in the small, nearby townships, not for tourists as they were at the bazaar in the city of Hotan.

Mehrigul was in the middle of rearranging the peaches yet again when she spotted a well-fed foreign lady wearing sunglasses and a wide-brimmed hat. She had on tan pants and a black, long-sleeved shirt that showed off her gold jewelry. Two large bags and a camera dangled from her shoulders. Mehrigul couldn't see her eyes, but she liked the easy smile on her lips.

"I'm glad you're back," the man who was with the lady said — in Uyghur, to Mehrigul's relief. "My name is Abdul, and this is Mrs. Chazen. Susan Chazen, from America."

"Hello," Mehrigul said, the English word she had practiced at school feeling strange in her mouth. "My name is Mehrigul." The lady held out her hand, forcing Mehrigul to come out from behind the cart, no matter how unsightly she was. They shook hands and nodded.

The lady with him, Abdul explained, was from San Francisco in the United States. She owned a craft shop and was on a buying trip. She was interested in purchasing the vine basket and wondered if Mehrigul had more.

"No more," Mehrigul told Abdul, "but it's only a basket made from grapevines." Her eyes darted from the vine basket to her grandfather's prized willow baskets. "There are grapevines everywhere," she said, amazed that anyone would want something so common. "I could make more, but are you certain she wouldn't rather have a willow basket?"

Abdul and Mrs. Chazen spoke together in rapid English that was far beyond Mehrigul's comprehension.

"It is your vine basket she wants," Abdul told her, "and as many more as you can make in any shape or form that pleases you. She thinks your work is very skillful. Mrs. Chazen is traveling to Kashgar but will return in three weeks. Can you meet us here at that time with whatever you have made?"

Mehrigul could not stop her lips from trembling. She didn't know whether she was holding back laughter or tears. Could she do it again? Make something the lady wanted? She hung her head but nodded yes. Her grandfather would help her. He would know what she had to do. It would no longer be play, but work.

"Mrs. Chazen would like to pay you for the basket and wonders if she might have the sprig of cotton, too. What is your price, Mehrigul?" Abdul asked.

"One yuan?" she whispered, then instantly wished she'd said less.

Again, Abdul spoke to Mrs. Chazen in a blur of words.

A slight smile was on Mrs. Chazen's lips as she took off her sunglasses and studied Mehrigul, her eyes neither friendly nor mean.

With a sudden gesture, the lady held up her hand and waved it back and forth. That meant one hundred yuan! *She knows our signs,* Mehrigul thought.

Or not. She must have made a mistake.

Mehrigul held her breath as Mrs. Chazen dug into one of her bags, knowing it couldn't be true. Until a crisp, fresh one-hundred-yuan note was thrust into her hand. She'd never held a hundred-yuan note before.

Even as she fingered it, stared at it, it was unreal. She'd never wished for or even dreamed about something like this.

Abdul touched her arm. "Mrs. Chazen is very pleased you agreed to sell your basket," he said, gently steering her toward the head of the cart. "I'll help you untie it."

Together they removed the basket. Mrs. Chazen wrapped it in soft white paper and placed it in her bag.

"Goodbye, Mehrigul," she said. "I'll be back."

"Good . . . bye," Mehrigul repeated, and watched them walk away. She was pleased that Mrs. Chazen's shoes were low-heeled, gray from a coat of dust. Not red, high-platform shoes, but the sensible shoes of someone who did not seem to care that Mehrigul looked like a peasant.

TWO

Ata made sad work of hitching their old donkey to the cart, fumbling and cursing as he tried to fit the poles through the loops of the harness. Mehrigul didn't offer to help. She set about arranging sacks of unsold peaches and baskets on their small cart to separate her from her father as much as possible—his legs hanging over the front, Mehrigul on the back edge, away from the reek of his breath. He'd spent their money on more than gambling.

No words were spoken. No scolding about the unsold peaches. Certainly no mention of the missing grapevine basket. Finally, a slap of Ata's willow whip on the donkey's backside sent the cart plowing into the pathway toward the exit.

"Posh! Posh!" Ata yelled, rudely making the other donkey carts and wagons give way. Mehrigul met the polite gestures of neighbors and friends with a tight smile as she retied her scarf under her chin. Surely Hajinsa would

think that appropriate for the daughter of a drunken peasant full of wine.

The road between the poplars narrowed as they came nearer to their farm. The only sounds now were the crunch of their wheels turning in the dirt, the croaking of frogs along the irrigation ditch, the rattling *ka, ka, ka* of cuckoos. Mehrigul was soothed by the cacophony of familiar sounds; at the same time, her mind was in battle. She reached deep into her pocket and touched her one-hundred-yuan note to be sure it was still there. That it was real. With her whole being she wanted to keep it secret from her father. She couldn't bear the thought of its being wasted on gambling or wine. But she knew she had to tell him.

"Ata?" Mehrigul said. A moan was his answer. Likely he'd fallen asleep. The donkey knew the way home and didn't need anyone to guide him.

"Ata."

"What ... what is it?" he finally said.

"Ana will be upset we didn't sell the peaches. We need the money." There was no reply. "The corn is still lying in the field. We should take it to the mill."

Ata waved his arm as if brushing away a pesky fly. "Mutalip will grind it," he mumbled. "I'll pay ... later."

Mehrigul recoiled at Ata's words. Mutalip was her best friend's father. Already generous to her family. How could Ata ask for more?

"You owe him money from before." Mehrigul spoke the words slowly and fiercely, as her hand dug into her pocket, pushing her note in deeper, farther away from her father.

Slowly Ata turned toward her, his head bobbing until his eyes focused. "If you'd sold the peaches, we'd have money to shell and grind the corn." The awful curl of his lips made Mehrigul shudder. Ata was sober enough to figure out how to blame her and make it seem he'd done nothing wrong at all.

But his words were true. Ata's offense didn't excuse her. Mehrigul felt ashamed that she, too, had let the family down.

"It's not something I do well — as you do, Ata." Mehrigul bowed her head as a swirl of memories swept over her. "Memet was good at selling," she said. "The girls brought their mothers and neighbors to buy from him." She stopped. Calling back those days was not helpful.

"That's why we always came home with an empty cart last summer," she added, her voice again under control.

Ata's head slumped to the side, his eyes taking on a blank stare. His mouth opened but he didn't speak.

"We all miss him. He'll be back soon, I'm sure," Mehrigul said, lying, once more guarding Memet's secret from Ata. Ata, who each day stood staring down the lane, hoping, expecting to see his son riding home on the back of someone's motorcycle.

They rode in silence for a few more minutes. Then Ata righted himself. Taking a big gulp of air, he slid from the cart and walked alongside, his stride unsure at first, then more and more firm.

"You will cut the peaches when we get home," he said. "Prepare them for drying. There should be room on the roof." For a brief moment he stopped walking. Then started again, pounding his feet into the dusty road. "I'll speak with your ana. It's best she doesn't see you preparing them. I'll drop my knife and the bags in the shed."

Again, Mehrigul let her fingers caress the crisp note. It would pay the fees and buy the clothes she and her little sister needed for school for the whole year and more. That was a nice dream, but it wouldn't keep them from going hungry during the winter months as their fields lay barren. She knew the money must go to Mutalip so they would have cornmeal for their naan and porridge. Was Ata thinking about the food they would need when he threw their money away on wine and gambling?

"Stop the cart, Ata." Mehrigul jumped down and held out the one-hundred-yuan note for him to see.

"Where'd you get that?" he said, his eyes narrowing. "What have you been hiding from me?" He lurched toward her.

"The . . . vine . . . basket," she stammered, inching backwards. "I . . . sold it."

Ata's eyes darted to the crossbar, then back to Mehrigul. "Yes?" he said, pointing his finger at the hundred yuan. "So?"

"A lady from America liked it . . . and bought it. I told her it would cost one yuan. She gave me one hundred."

"For that basket?" Ata said. His hands went to his hips. He was shaking his head. Almost laughing.

Then his hand cupped his beard. He stepped closer. "What else does she want from you?"

"I . . . I don't know. She was pleased with my basket. She wants me to make more." Mehrigul clasped her hands to stop the shaking. She hadn't thought there could be anything wrong with selling the basket. "She'll return to the market in three weeks to buy others that I make."

Ata's brows drew together, his eyes clear now and black as coal.

"A Uyghur man was with her," Mehrigul said, trying

to stand straighter and taller than she was feeling. "He seemed nice, too . . . and I thought if I could make more baskets and sell them . . . it would help."

Mehrigul could not tell what Ata was thinking as he scowled at her.

"I promise I won't take time away from chores," she said. "I know how much must be done. I'll do everything you tell me."

Ata's face darkened. She wanted to run from him. She knew he was a good father, a good man. But lately — since Memet left — with his drinking, his thinking was not right.

The money was what he looked at now, not her.

"Take it," Mehrigul said, holding the money out, her head bent. She must not let him see the ill will that boiled inside her, the mistrust that would show in her eyes. "It should be enough to pay our debt and have our corn shelled and ground." She tried to make her voice even and steady. "I'll ask Pati and her brother to come with their wagon to carry it to the mill."

Still Ata glared at the note. Was he thinking what she was, that selling the peaches wouldn't have brought in nearly enough yuan to do that?

"We don't need to tell Ana what happened today," Mehrigul said, fighting back tears. But she couldn't stop herself from saying more. "All the money must go to Mutalip for the corn," she said as she thrust the note into his palm. "If there's any left, it's to be used for Lali's school fees and clothes so she'll look decent."

Ata gaped, then slowly closed his mouth to a straight, hard line. His eyes flared as he grabbed the money and jammed it into his pocket. "I will decide what's to be done!"

He turned and stomped to the cart. He flicked the willow whip at the donkey, who took off at a trot.

Mehrigul stood frozen. She had bad feelings about what had just happened. And she wondered why, for that fleeting moment, the hundred yuan had given her the power to be disrespectful.

As she stared at her empty hands, she understood. When she handed Ata the money, it was as if she was throwing away all hope of being in charge of her own future. A silly hope — she knew a hundred yuan was not enough to give her choices.

Mehrigul watched the cart grow smaller and smaller, then ran, straining every muscle, stirring her own cloud of dust as she rushed to catch up. The old donkey jerked his head when she reached the cart. He knew Mehrigul was there. So did Ata, but he did not acknowledge her.

"I'm sorry," Mehrigul said, struggling for breath. "I

shouldn't have said that. You know what is best to do with the money." Her arms hung at her sides as she labored to keep pace with the cart. "Please, Ata, give me permission to make more baskets. We need the money. When the lady comes back, you'll see she's honorable."

Ata slowed the donkey to a walk. Twisted his head to look at her. "You think she'll come back, do you? People like that don't keep their word." He spat at the ground. "Besides, what makes you think one hundred yuan is so special? Girls working in factories around here make that much every month. I could lie about your age."

Ata picked up his whip and hit the donkey's rump. "It's men who are craftsmen, not women," he said. "Don't you dare waste your time on something so foolish. Dreamers like you are cleaved like an apple and thrown to the desert."

Mehrigul knew the proverb. She had no expectations that following a dream would lead to anything useful. She ran to catch the edge of the cart and pulled herself on as Ata gave the donkey another lashing.

"You're nothing but a peasant — and don't forget it, as your brother did," he called back over his shoulder, his voice louder with every word.

Ata was right. She had been foolish. Foolish enough to believe that the American lady really did want to buy her baskets, and that she could make more that the lady would like. Especially foolish to presume that knowing Ata's secret, and earning her own money, gave her some kind of privilege.

She leaned her head against the bag that held her grandfather's baskets.

Yet, in her belly, she sensed something new, something she couldn't let pass by.

A stranger had thought her simple twist of vines to be of value.

THREE

THE CHILL OF AUTUMN was in the air as Mehrigul carried the last batch of peaches up the ladder to the roof. There'd been no call for help to prepare supper or to bring her grandfather to the evening meal. Her mother must have been told she was busy with chores. The sun had already joined the earth. It was past time to eat.

Hunger hadn't been on Mehrigul's mind. The juicy pulp of yet one more peach stopped the rumble in her stomach. She went now to the front yard and rubbed her hands clean in the cold water from the spigot. She cupped her hands and splashed her face, letting the water drip over her shirt and vest.

Still dripping, Mehrigul stood in the doorway, her eyes adjusting to the dim light of the oil lamp. Ata and the others sat cross-legged on the floor rugs, drinking tea. Broken pieces of naan lay scattered on the eating cloth; there was a bit of *polo* on the platter.

Lali ran to Mehrigul. How good it was to have her

sister's arms squeeze her in greeting. "Oooh, you're wet," Lali said, as quickly pulling away.

Ana scraped what was left of the rice mixture into a bowl and set it in front of Mehrigul's eating place. "Tea?" she asked.

"Yes . . . please." Mehrigul was surprised at Ana's attention. She was used to doing these things herself.

Then she wondered if drinking warm tea was worth having to sit across from Ata. She wouldn't look at him, but it was clear from Ana's calm that they'd all been told of a successful day at market. Ata's version. Whatever lie he'd made up.

The strong, rich odor of mutton fat overruled her anger. Mehrigul scooped the rice into her mouth with her fingers. There was more fat than usual in tonight's *polo*, but no pieces of mutton. The dark specks were raisins.

It was Ata's habit to bring home a small packet of mutton on market days. Memet had done this when he was in charge of going to market. Had Ata forgotten, or had he drunk and gambled away all the pitiful earnings he'd pocketed before wandering off? If her mother thought they'd sold their goods, wouldn't she ask why Ata hadn't brought meat? Mehrigul hoped she wouldn't be called upon to explain.

She leaned back, for the first time slowing her eating.

"You were hungry, Daughter," Ana said.

Ana had been watching. Everyone had been watching.

She straightened up, licked her fingers. "I had two eggs. Your friend the egg woman kindly gave them to me in exchange for peaches. Remember her, Ana?" Mehrigul turned toward her mother. "You used to be friends. She doesn't even ask about you anymore."

Ana's head dropped onto her chest. Mehrigul's words had been unkind, but they were true, and for some reason she couldn't hold them back tonight. If Ana were doing the work she was supposed to, Mehrigul might still be able to go to school. Many wives tended the goods from their farm at market. But Ana was too ashamed to be seen with their old donkey and cart, too ashamed to be seen in the washed-out clothing she wore. It had become Memet's job three years ago, when he was old enough to go, while Ana stayed home wallowing in remembrance of the happy, comfortable childhood she had lived in her village.

"How is Aynurkhan? It has been a long . . ." Ana's voice trailed off.

"She still sits by the pots and pans, the same busy spot." Mehrigul's words were slow and deliberate. She wanted Ata to hear what she was saying — wanted him to know that she had been only a few meters away from where he was gambling. Would he wonder if she'd seen him? She hoped so.

"Hajinsa was there, too," she went on, "perched on a mat she'd bought. Eating one egg after another as if she were an imperial princess." Mehrigul extended her arm with the grace of a heron taking flight, her fingers rippling the air in imitation of Hajinsa picking at the eggshell. "So, you see, Ana, not much was talked of with Aynurkhan."

Lali giggled as her arms fluttered in imitation of her sister.

With a sharp look at Mehrigul, Ata rose, and the moment of lightness passed. He'd heard her words. He knew that the egg seller sat near the gambling table. Still, he couldn't know whether or not she'd seen him. Mehrigul was sure Ata would never ask her about that.

Ata's uncertainty would just be another reason why she and her father were not comfortable together. They never had been. Memet was all to Ata—his only son, the perfect one. Mehrigul was useful at times, dutiful, swift in her tasks, but dreamy, Ata complained. Distracted by the shapes and sounds of things, by her private thoughts.

Like now. Ata had been speaking and her mind was far

away. Ana would have to relay Mehrigul's list of chores for the morning.

"... to the mill," he said, "after the wheat is planted."

Mehrigul hoped that meant she might go to the mill to make arrangements to have the corn ground. She could see Pati. There was much to tell, and much to ask.

"Did you hear me, Mehrigul?" Ata's voice was hard-edged. "We get started at sunrise."

There was strained silence in the room as Ata went to the door.

Only when Ata had returned from outside and gone to his sleeping platform did Mehrigul pick up her half-eaten piece of naan and dip it into her tepid tea. She leaned back on her haunches and sucked on it, drawing out as much of the oniony flavor as possible.

Her full belly, the dim light, the heat still radiating from their small cooking stove, made Mehrigul sleepy. She finished her tea and abruptly stood. "I'll help Chong Ata," she said. Her grandfather was squatting across from her, a small bundle of old bones and sagging flesh. Hard of hearing, his eyesight poor.

Aside from Lali, Chong Ata was the person she cared most about. She'd sat at his side by the hour from the time she was a small child. One by one, she'd handed him willow branches for his baskets as he crouched on the dirt floor of his workroom. She had nestled her bare feet next to his as he held down the branches to build a base. Watched as he wove the sides and lashed the rim. She'd learned to make her own little baskets. In time, she had been allowed to help make the baskets that went to market. Her fingers were shaped like Chong Ata's. Not long and slender like Hajinsa's but nimble and knowing like her grandfather's.

Mehrigul went to his side. "Time to go to sleep, Chong Ata," she said, leaning over to speak close to his ear.

He reached for her arm and leaned against her as she rocked him to an upright position.

She helped him step into his shoes and led him to the yard so he could relieve himself. Then they went to his workroom. It was the only place her grandfather would sleep.

"Good night, Chong Ata," she said as she covered him with the felt rug.

Tomorrow, when no one was around to overhear, she would tell him about the grapevine basket.

FOUR

MEHRIGUL GLIDED OVER THE open field as quietly as the morning mist, liking the blanket of cold dampness that engulfed her, the soft, shrouded light of the sun rising in its filmy haze. She'd left her sleeping platform, thrown on pants and shirt, and stolen from the house before Ana could call her to do breakfast chores. Lali was old enough to help.

If Mehrigul went early to the field and prepared it for planting, there might be time at the end of the day to steal away and gather vines. And if she did? A tightness gripped her body. Could she really make another basket like the one the woman had bought?

The thought was unsettling, yet her fingers danced in eagerness to try, even as she cleared the field of leftover ears of corn and carried them to the large pile of cobs that had been gathered for the mill. Scattered stalks needed to be picked up, too. What they didn't need themselves could be sold at market as fodder and bedding.

Mehrigul had begun to hoe seedbeds for the planting when Ana came onto the field, the seed bag hanging from her waist. Every step she took told of her weariness, of the place she'd withdrawn to so no more unhappiness could reach her.

"Where's Ata?" Mehrigul said. "I have Memet's hoe. Why isn't Ata here with his hoe to help?" She lashed the words that had festered in her head at Ana, who clutched her arms in front of her.

"Why . . . he has gone to see Mutalip . . . to arrange for him to pick up our corn." Her bewildered eyes darted over Mehrigul's face. "Surely you understood . . . you and I are to plant . . ." Ana lowered her head. "We had best get busy," she said.

"Yes, Ana. Sorry. I should have been listening to what he said."

Mehrigul lowered Memet's hoe to the large field of un-turned earth that stretched before her. She dug down — not too deep, not too shallow — and began again to furrow the seedbed for their crop of winter wheat. "I told him I'd arrange for Pati's brother to carry our corn to the mill," she said. "I thought Ata would help so the planting could get done before the warmth of the day dried out the topsoil."

If Ana heard, she didn't answer. She kept moving

with measured pace, doubled over at the waist, dropping pinches of seeds inch by inch along the prepared rows.

Ana didn't seem to mind that Ata had abandoned them, but Mehrigul did. Her grip tightened with each jab of the hoe, the splintery wood boring into her palms until the pain brought her to reality. She couldn't twist and weave unwieldy vines into something of importance with injured hands. Blisters had already begun to form on her hands. She didn't want to make them worse.

Right now Mehrigul must focus only on the long task ahead. It seemed likely that Ana knew nothing about the unsold peaches or the magical appearance of one hundred yuan — or didn't want to know. Ata was faultless. Surely, she thought bitterly, it was his job to drive off in the donkey cart and spend her money while they worked the field.

It was midafternoon before the last row was turned, seeded, and firmly covered with soil. In a rare moment of usefulness, Ana had noticed Mehrigul's red, swollen fingers and offered to switch tasks, relieving her own tired back, too.

As they returned to the house, neither ana nor daughter spoke of the corn pile that still loomed at the side of the yard. When Mehrigul hung the hoe and seed bag in the shed, it was no surprise to her that the donkey and cart were not there. Ata used to go to the steam baths in the nearby township once or twice a week — Memet, too, when they were both working hard on the farm. Surely that was where he had gone, in tribute to the hard work his wife and daughter were doing. And then out drinking, to be certain he didn't return home before their job was done.

Ana wouldn't question him. She'd fold her hands meekly in front of her and do his bidding. Try not to draw back if he stank of wine.

Maybe Ata was out gambling away the hundred yuan — and Mehrigul wouldn't say anything, either. It was his money now. Somehow, though, she'd make baskets, get them to market, and keep the money next time. She'd use it to help her family.

Another thought came to Mehrigul as she swooped up an armful of dry twigs and headed for the house. The men Ata drank and gambled with — had they sent their daughters to work so they'd have more money? Was that what Ata was doing? Finding out how to lie about her age, how to get false identification papers that claimed she was sixteen rather than fourteen? It could be done. She'd had a friend at school whose family sent her to work in the local cotton factory before she was of age.

One hundred yuan? Nothing, he'd said. Mehrigul

would be a *real* help if she went to work — and brought money home to Ata.

She snapped the twigs she'd brought inside into small pieces and stuffed them into the round metal cookstove that sat atop a small tripod stand. She grabbed the kettle and headed for the spigot in the yard. Brought it back. Set it to boil.

Ana was resting.

What would the family do without Mehrigul right now? Was Ata thinking about that? All her jobs would fall to Ana. Even if she earned money, someone would have to do the work. Couldn't Ata tell she was doing all she could to take Memet's place?

Mehrigul was on her way to bring Chong Ata in for tea when the neighbor's donkey cart stopped out on the road, delivering Lali from her day at school. How lucky that the neighbors were glad to have Lali's company for their daughter, now that Mehrigul no longer went to school.

What if she couldn't be here to welcome Lali home?

For a moment she stood paralyzed. Finally she forced a smile as her sister skipped across the yard toward her.

She engulfed Lali with hungry, outstretched arms. Held her as her mind tried to dismiss any thoughts of Ata's treachery. He wouldn't make her go away! Would he?

Lali wiggled free from Mehrigul's hold. "*Xiang bu xiang qu tiao wu?*" she asked in Mandarin as she spun in circles, grabbing at Mehrigul's hands, trying to turn her around in circles, too.

Mehrigul hated the pinched, nasal sounds of Mandarin. "Would I like to go dancing?" she repeated in Uyghur, drawing out the soft, lyrical sounds of the words. Hearing her little sister speak the language of their oppressors unsettled her. She didn't want to hear it. Not now. Not ever.

But it was the language spoken in school, and in all important places. Lali had to know it. Mehrigul had to know it.

Lali stood in front of Mehrigul now, tapping her foot, her head tilted, waiting for her sister's answer.

"*Xie xie*, thank you, Lali. It's a good thing for us to do," Mehrigul said. She grabbed Lali's hands and twirled her round and round. Soon they were laughing and skipping and dancing, stirring up the packed earth of their grassless yard.

"*Ke yi. Gou la.* Okay. Enough," Mehrigul said as she pinned her sister's hands together and pulled her to a halt.

"No," Lali moaned. "Dancing is fun."

"And we have things to do. Time to take Chong Ata

in for tea and to help Ana with supper," Mehrigul said, turning Lali around in the direction of their house.

Lali broke away, running into her grandfather's room. "*Wo men he cha ba, Yeye.* Let's have some tea, Grandfather," she'd called in Mandarin before Mehrigul could stop her.

Chong Ata had heard. His hand went up, cupping his mouth as he turned his head away.

Mehrigul drew Lali back into the yard. Waited until her sister's eyes met hers. "Mandarin is our secret language here at home, Lali. Remember? Chong Ata and Ata and Ana don't understand the words, and they don't want to learn. It upsets them if we speak anything but Uyghur." Mehrigul tightened her grip as she saw her sister's lips begin to quiver. "No, Lali, you must understand. Hearing Mandarin reminds them of how different their lives were before the Han Chinese overran our land. We must not be the ones who remind them."

She put her arm around Lali's shoulder, gently pushing her down until they were squatting side by side in the yard.

"When Chong Ata was a young boy, his country was called East Turkestan. Mostly Uyghurs lived here. But you won't learn that in school, Lali," Mehrigul said, her voice losing its gentleness. "The Chinese act as if they've always been here, that it's always been their land. Chong Ata won't even talk about the past anymore. It's too sad for him." Mehrigul struggled to hold back her anger; she didn't want to frighten Lali.

"When I was very little, Ata's brother, Uncle Kasim, and his family lived with us on the farm. I remember dancing and singing right here in our yard with aunts and uncles and cousins." Mehrigul swirled her hand around in the layer of dust and sand that covered their hard-baked yard. There had been many celebrations here at festival and holiday times, Chong Ata used to tell her, as Chong Ata's father and grandfather had told him.

"I'd like to have cousins and friends living with me," Lali said, nestling against Mehrigul. "We could dance and sing together all the time. Maybe they wouldn't always be as busy as you are."

"Maybe not, Lali," Mehrigul said, hugging her sister closer. "But our farm couldn't feed so many people anymore. The Chinese began taking over the land and misusing our precious water supply. Uncle Kasim became a cook and moved his family to a city far away." Now Memet was gone too.

"Why are the Chinese so mean?" Lali asked.

For a moment, Mehrigul was silent. She wanted to tell Lali, wanted her to understand, but the truth could be dangerous for her sister to know. "You must never repeat what I'm going to tell you — not to your teachers or to your friends. This is secret between us," she said, keeping her voice as steady and calm as she could. "It's because they don't want us here. We're in their way, and we don't talk and think and do things the way they do.

"Like right now." Mehrigul rose, pulling Lali with her. "You're going into Chong Ata's room, and in your most beautiful Uyghur you will invite him to tea, which he will drink while sitting on a Uyghur rug on our dirt floor."

There was little naan left to go with their tea. Ana would have to bake again, and it had become Mehrigul's chore to prepare their outdoor earth oven. She gathered wood that would burn down to the hot coals needed to bake the bread. As she tended the fire, she dug a few carrots, radishes, and turnips from the garden for soup.

Tasks done, Mehrigul walked across their fields into the peach orchard. A large patch of grapevines lay beyond. Overgrown, neglected, but useful for the meager crop of grapes they harvested and dried for raisins. And suitable for basket making. Autumn was a good season for gathering branches, Chong Ata always said.

Mehrigul ran her hands through the tangled thicket of bushes until she found a vine the size she wanted. She pulled it free, stretching it out well over an arm's length. She tested it, wrapping it around her fist. It did not splinter or break, so it was supple enough to be woven. There would be no time for seasoning the stems as Chong Ata did with the willow he used, drying them and then resoaking them. The vines she picked must be used right away. In less than three weeks Mrs. Chazen would return.

Mehrigul twisted and bent and ripped at the branch, but she could not break it loose. She should have known there was no way to harvest vine shoots without a knife. She wanted only the small, perfect part of each branch.

There were three knives in the family: Ana's cooking knife; Ata's, which he always carried; and Chong Ata's, which he used to cut and shape willow branches. There had been a fourth — Memet's, the one that cut the grapevines for Mrs. Chazen's basket.

Mehrigul sank to the ground. Where was Memet now when she needed him so badly?

* * *

Mehrigul remembered the night her brother left. It was late August, just before school was to begin. She had heard the roar and sputter of a motorcycle coming down the roadway, bringing Memet home. He'd been spending more and more time with friends, hanging out in cafés, sometimes as far away as Hotan. Ata didn't like the boys who picked him up on their motorcycles. He was afraid Memet would get into trouble in their company.

Ata had yelled at Memet when he came through the door. Memet didn't say anything. He got the *rawap* from its peg on the wall, sat cross-legged on the floor, and began to play and sing.

> *I invited a guest into my home*
> *Asked him to sit in the place of honor*
> *But my guest never left*
> *Now he's made my home his own*

Mehrigul hoped Memet hadn't sung this song in front of a Chinese person who understood Uyghur; the guest who would never leave was the Han Chinese.

Memet stopped singing but his fingers still plucked at the strings, the notes sliding in and out of shifting scales. "We Uyghurs are slaves to the Han," he declared. "There's no place for us here anymore."

The notes had slowed to a fragile, mournful sound that seemed to come from Memet's heart. "There is no place for *me* here," he said. "I must know what else is out there, where my hope lies.

"I'll be back," he'd said. "Someday."

Sleep had not come to Mehrigul that night. Maybe she'd known there would be no other goodbye from Memet — that he would not be there in the morning. She hadn't been surprised to hear a scuffling of feet on their earthen floor, the creak of door hinges. She'd bolted from her platform and followed him, not caring that she was in her sleep clothes.

"Memet. Wait," she'd whispered loudly, running to catch up with him.

He stopped but did not turn to look at her.

Mehrigul grabbed his arm. Felt him shaking. He put his hand over hers and led her to the road where his friend was waiting, standing beside his silent motorcycle.

"Yusup, this is my sister," Memet said.

"*Salam*," his friend replied, making no effort to hide his impatience. "Memet, we must leave. Let's go."

"No." The firmness in her own voice startled her. Something bad had happened. She had to know.

Memet held his palm out to Yusup. "She'll keep our

secret," he said as he bent toward her. "But no one, not Ata, *no one* must know what I'm telling you. They must only know I've left. If Ata tries to find out whether they've captured me, he'll get in trouble. End up in prison himself."

Then Memet told her about the demonstration. Memet, Yusup, more than a hundred other boys, men — even women and children, he'd said — had gathered at the Hotan market for a peaceful protest. They hated that they'd lost their farms just because the Han wanted them. His friend Jawab and his ata had refused to give up their land and had been taken away to some unknown prison. It was an innocent protest. They weren't armed. Memet said the police had attacked them before they got started. Shot at them. Killed at least twenty. Injured more.

"We've got to go, little sister," Yusup said to Mehrigul, grabbing the handlebars of his motorcycle. Beginning to push it down the road. "By now they'll have the roads blocked and be looking for us. Our pictures could be on their cameras."

Memet's arms engulfed her, lifted her from the ground in an almost strangling embrace. Then Memet and Yusup were shoving the motorcycle down a narrow trail, away from the main road. A path that would, before dawn, lead them to the desert's edge.

FIVE

The grapevine was still entwined around Mehrigul's hand as she stirred from her memories. Someone was calling. Not Ana, but a voice she knew. Her friend Pati. She rose and slowly untangled herself from the vine as she tried to clear her thoughts.

Her friend's red jacket was the first thing she saw as she threaded her way back through the peach orchard. Pati always wore red — a beacon of happiness. Always smiling, safe in a family of grandparents, parents who adored her, a brother, a sister, aunts, uncles, little ones.

Mehrigul thought Pati's happiness also came from the rushing stream that flowed through the mill beside her home, powering the turbine that moved the huge stone circles to grind wheat or corn. Mehrigul had been known to sit for hours watching the gushing water. She'd gladly be transported there now, but she saw Ata shoveling corncobs onto the wagon Pati and her brother had brought over from the mill. Ana was helping. Even Lali.

Pati walked across the field toward Mehrigul, who slowed her steps. She wanted as much time as possible with her friend before going back to work.

They greeted with a hug, Pati not seeming to mind that Mehrigul was grubby and smelly from her day's labor.

"I brought a book, Mehrigul," Pati said. "Lessons are difficult this year." She shrugged. "You wouldn't think so, but I do. I need your help . . . I miss you."

Mehrigul reached for Pati's hands and pressed them. She averted her eyes to shield her friend from the bitterness that swelled within her — anger that she couldn't pursue studies that would give her some chance for her future.

They began to walk toward the house. "I'll have very little time for us to be together." Mehrigul's words were muted. "There's much to do here."

"I'll ride my bicycle over after school. That will give us some time," Pati said.

"I can't explain, but I won't be able to see you for a few weeks."

"Does your ata make you do everything Memet used to do? You already had a lot of chores of your own."

"There's another thing I must do now, too. It's important. And . . ." Mehrigul halted. "Are you still studying English?"

"You're acting crazy, Mehrigul. There's something so important you can't see me. Then, suddenly, you're interested in English."

Mehrigul hung her head. "I can't talk about it."

"Well," Pati said, "since you asked, there is someone who comes to our class to teach us English once a week. Our teacher wants to learn, and she makes us do it too."

Mehrigul nodded, then quickened her step. "I must help with the corn," she said. "Ata keeps glaring at me."

"Let the others work. You're treated like a drudge around here when you should take care of yourself and think about finding a good husband." Pati's face turned as red as her jacket.

"So, all goes well with you and Azat?" Mehrigul asked.

Pati sighed as her face turned a deeper shade of crimson.

"I'm happy for you, Pati," Mehrigul said. "But that's not for me." She would not spoil her friend's contentment by saying that the last thing in the world she, Mehrigul, dreamed of was moving into another household to work for someone else, even if it were her husband. She turned away. There was more. "Things are not good for my family right now," she added in a hushed voice, overcome for the moment by the divide that was growing between her life and Pati's. Wondering what it meant.

Pati's arm locked around Mehrigul's waist as they moved toward the corn pile, and Mehrigul let herself enjoy the comfort of knowing she had no reason to question her friend's loyalty. Yet she also knew that she would no longer share her deepest fears — like being sent away by Ata — with her friend. Was she too ashamed to tell her? Or afraid Pati would desert her? Was she shutting herself off from the world as Ana had done?

"I bet I can load more corncobs onto that wagon than you can, and do it faster," Pati said.

For now, anyway, Mehrigul and Pati were in step, and it felt good.

Pati and Azat, the felt maker's son, would marry, Mehrigul thought as they hurried along; they had already been promised. A match between these two Uyghur families — the miller's daughter and the felt maker's son — would be a good one. Azat would take his father's place as master felt maker one day. It was a fine business. Their rugs were sold for high prices to the Chinese and to the tourists who shopped at the covered mall in Hotan.

Pati wouldn't be allowed to make rugs. She wouldn't choose the colors or patterns. She'd heat the water that must be sprinkled over the wool at just the right moment. Mehrigul had watched Azat and his family make rugs, and that was the role of his mother. And would someday be the role of his wife. She'd bear his children, cook, sew.

She'd always wear red and would never be hungry.

Mehrigul's arm encircled Pati. She was happy for her friend.

For herself? She saw no contentment in such a future. Going to school had been her hope and joy. If she studied hard, spoke perfect Mandarin, maybe she could get a job at the museum in Hotan. That was her dream. Mehrigul wanted to be the person telling visitors that her Uyghur ancestors had been here greeting people during the golden age of the old Silk Road.

That dream was beyond her reach now. But a new dream stirred in her, one that brought fear as well as pleasure. There was something she wanted more desperately as each day passed — to make another basket worthy of Mrs. Chazen's attention.

For the next three weeks Mehrigul would allow herself only that one thought. No matter what happened after, she'd have this special moment in time.

SIX

I<small>T WAS PAST NOON</small> when Ata announced he would go to the mill to collect the bags of ground corn. Ana went to the orchard to gather the last of the peaches, overripe now, not suitable for sale at market. She would dry them. A few, she promised, would be made into peach juice — a treat for the family. Mehrigul was to help Chong Ata.

She went to his workroom and knelt quietly at his side, watching his hands build the core for a new basket. She thought to move him out to the yard, into the sun, for the earthen floor of his room was cold and unwelcoming. But he was deep at work — his hands, not his eyes, guiding his movements. His hands still made good baskets, but they seemed no longer to be infused with the creative spark that once set his weaving apart from others', making his baskets the most highly valued at market. Perhaps Chong Ata knew this.

The core completed, Mehrigul handed Chong Ata a willow branch from the pile that lay beside him. She watched as he wove the shoot in and out of the long willow rods that spread from the core, waiting to hand him the next branch.

"I have news, Chong Ata," she said, "that will surprise you, as much as it surprised me."

Chong Ata nodded. He had heard. "Yes?" he said.

"I made a grapevine basket last summer that Memet and I tied on the donkey cart. A foreign lady at the market bought it . . . and she wants more." Mehrigul hesitated. "Is it wrong for a girl to make baskets? Ata said it's only men who are the craftsmen."

A smile crossed Chong Ata's face. He stopped weaving. Held his work upright with his bare feet as he reached for Mehrigul's hands. Stroked her fingers.

"It is the tradition of our people that men carry on the craft of their fathers, but it is you who have magic fingers, Granddaughter. A special gift. I have watched you. It is you who could carry on the family tradition, not your father or Memet. I'm pleased that you felt ready to make your own kind of basket. I'm proud of you."

"But Chong Ata," she said, "I don't know what to do. I don't even have a knife to work with. Even if I did, I'm not certain I can make anything else that's good, that the lady will like. And I don't know when I'll find time. The new baskets must be ready in less than three weeks."

"You will borrow my knife," Chong Ata said. He reached inside his coat and pulled his knife from its battered leather sheath, his Yengisar knife. It had been hand-crafted in the town of Yengisar, where for hundreds of years the secrets and techniques of making these knives had been passed down from generation to generation, from father to son. It was the most simple and beautiful knife Mehrigul had ever seen. The finely etched pattern on the brass handle, the silver blade, spoke of the skillful Uyghur craftsman who had made it.

"Use it now," Chong Ata said. "I can do without it for the rest of the day."

Mehrigul bowed as he passed it to her and kept her head low as she forced her next words out. "Ana does not know about my basket . . . and I can't tell her. And Ata . . . he must not know that I'm doing this work."

"There is trouble?" Chong Ata asked.

"I can't explain, but please don't say anything."

Before going to the grape patch, Mehrigul went inside the house to Ana's sewing box. She cut off a thin strip of white cotton cloth — so little that Ana couldn't possibly no-tice — and hid it and the sheathed knife in the deep pocket of her pants. To avoid meeting Ana, she walked down the lane to the back of their land.

On the right-hand side, across from the grapevine patch, was an old, neglected stand of bamboo that seemed to belong to no one. It had been a secret hiding place for Mehrigul and Memet when they were young children. No one could find them when they snuck deep inside and sat in the small clearing they made. She would go there now to tie her cloth.

It was more difficult than she remembered to push her way through the thicket of bamboo culms, some tall and straight and as stiff as small tree trunks, others slender, arched and supple. The old, broken culms tripped her and blocked her passage, but she soon found the special place she and Memet had made. It was overgrown now, and she pulled and tugged until she had made a small clearing to mark the spot again.

Mehrigul took the cloth from her pocket and held it close to her heart as she searched for the right culm. The bamboo would carry her wish, for there was no tamarisk tree nearby where she could leave her cloth. The tama-risk held more power than the bamboo. Like her Uyghur people, it knew how to survive the drifting sands of the desert, the tree's deep roots anchoring it against the fierce winds. For now, though, it was the power of the secret place she had shared with her brother that she must trust.

She chose a tall, slender culm, one that reminded her of a willowy branch of tamarisk. She tied her strip of cloth — her token — to the topmost part of the culm so that it would sway in the breeze, the better to be seen by God.

"Please send me the favor that my hands might make beautiful work. I want to make something special. And . . . please give me the courage to carry on," Mehrigul whispered, then stood in silence. Not because she believed God would listen to her and give her an answer but because she felt so at one with her people, who believed in the power of such tokens.

Mehrigul knew that if she was to fulfill her prayer, she must be like a stem that swayed with the winds; she must learn to bend but not break. To yield, and yet endure.

SEVEN

MEHRIGUL QUICKLY FOUND THE grapevine branch she'd tucked back into the thicket. She pulled it full length and cut it from the trunk. With a deftness that surprised her, she trimmed away the leaves and outgrowths, knowing that the sharpness of Chong Ata's knife made it possible but pleased at her own skillfulness with the knife. She searched for branches that same size and kept cutting and trimming until she had collected an ample bundle. Then she made another, less tidy pile: thick branches for handles, skinny ones for braiding.

"Now what, Mehrigul?" she asked herself.

She sat between the bundles and lowered her head to her knees.

She had no memory of how she'd begun the cone-shaped basket. Memet had handed her a few pieces of vine. Her fingers had just worked and twined and twisted and woven until there it was — a basket that held a stem of cotton bolls and decorated the cart.

Her hands were unsteady as she reached to pull five branches from the pile. She laid them in front of her. Studied them. Ran her fingers along the stems. Nothing but long, brown sticks, she thought, with joints every so often where there had been leaves or smaller branches. Here and there a springy tendril grew from a joint. She'd been careful not to cut the tendrils off, thinking they would add charm to her basket.

She stroked the branches.

She closed her eyes and stroked them.

No magic came.

She opened her eyes again and still saw nothing but plain branches. She also saw that the sun was fast approaching the tops of the Kunlun mountains, or that part of the sky where she knew the tops to be. The wind had come up, blowing a sandy haze across the oasis, half hiding the sun, which sank lower and lower. It would soon disappear, and there would be no more time for her to work.

Mehrigul put all she'd learned from Chong Ata out of her mind. Picked up five branches and folded them in half. She cut a piece from the thinnest vine she'd gathered and tied it around the bottom fold so they would stay together. Then she laid the branches out on the ground. There were now ten rods stretched out from the center tie, looking like a big spider web. Mehrigul took her shoes off and used her bare feet to help hold the rods down in an even pattern. Her feet were smaller than Chong Ata's, but they served the purpose.

She needed some kind of core before she began to weave the sides. Even spider webs had a kind of center. Taking short pieces of thin vine, she began to tie the rods together two by two. She changed the pattern when she made a second round, tying rod two to three, four to five, until she came to ten and one. On the third round she went back to one and two together, three and four together, until she came again to nine and ten.

Enough core, she decided. She bent the branches skyward and wrapped her legs around them, holding them up. She grabbed two long vines and, using them together, began to weave them in and out of the ten rods that would frame her basket. She worked fast, spreading the rods slightly each time she went around. Picking up new weavers as she needed them.

Mehrigul worked at a frenzied pace. Not stopping. Trying not to think about whether what she was doing was good or bad. Her hands seemed to go wild again as they had that day with Memet, knowing what they needed to do to make a basket that was good for nothing but to look at.

She loved it when the wispy tendrils showed up, looking like wiry worms sticking out from the sides of the basket.

When the top of her basket was as wide as her spread-out hand, she paused. Picked the basket up, turned it back and forth. It was cone-shaped, like the other one. Absolutely good for nothing. But hadn't Mrs. Chazen given her one hundred yuan for just such a useless thing?

Tomorrow she'd borrow Chong Ata's knife again. Trim and bind the basket. Add a small handle. Then make another that had some purpose — one that could hold peaches and still be a bit different. She'd try to do that.

She gathered her bundles of cut vines and took them to the bamboo grove. Her work must be kept as secret as her token. Going deep inside, she laid the vines at the side of her clearing, between sturdy stalks that would protect them from the wind and the sand. She brought in her unfinished basket, then covered everything with a few old and broken culms that lay scattered on the ground. No one ever came to the bamboo grove, but just in case . . .

Before Mehrigul started down the lane, she gathered a few bunches of leftover grapes she'd found hidden deep in the vines. She picked up fallen walnuts along the way and added them to the pouch she'd made from her shirt-tail. This would be the excuse for her absence — she'd been foraging for food. The grapes, when dried, would make a few more handfuls of raisins for them to eat during the winter. She'd crack open the walnuts and add the meats to their supper.

A smile crossed her face as she took one last look back at the bamboo grove.

Now both she and Ata had secrets.

EIGHT

PLEASE, ANA, GO WITH Ata to market. Just this once. You may have some friends left who'll stop by when they hear about your baked squash. What am I supposed to tell them when they ask for you? 'Where's Aynisa?' they'll say."

Ana had wandered over to the earth oven where Mehrigul stood, perhaps having some recollection that she should be useful.

Ana gave no response, nor had Mehrigul expected one.

Mehrigul was waiting for the last batch to be baked before loading it onto the donkey cart. She had started the baking the day before. The squash crop was abundant this year, and now was the perfect time for harvest. They should make good money today.

It was Mehrigul's task to build the fire in the bottom of the pit and to keep adding wood until it burned down to glowing hot coals. She covered the coals with a thick layer of green twigs to form a nest for the squash she had picked and washed. The squash were large, so only two or three fit in the oven at a time. Ana managed to appear when it was time to throw in her special ingredients — wild onions and a weed she never named but that she said had been used by her family since far back in time. The pit was covered by more green twigs and a layer of flat stones and left for hours.

With that batch cooked, Mehrigul would start over. She had worked late into the night and had begun again before dawn. Soon Ata would harness the donkey and it would be time to leave.

"Ana, please," Mehrigul pleaded again. If Ana went, she'd have many hours to make baskets, with no fear of being seen or called upon to work. And she hated the thought of being alone with Ata.

Ana stood with her hands clasped, her head slightly bowed. It had been years since she'd gone to market. Mehrigul knew Ana was embarrassed by their poverty. Most of all, she could not bear the pity of family and friends when she had no gifts to bring to them on birthdays or at weddings or funerals. She had no more pieces of the precious cotton she had brought with her from her village to give away when she made visits, and was too ashamed to go empty-handed. She no longer went gifting and wanted no one to bring a gift to her, for she could not spare the few nuts, or sugar cubes, or small loaves of naan she was expected to give in return. Ana no longer belonged to the world she'd once known and had withdrawn into a bleak and colorless existence. Mehrigul wondered if she even remembered why she didn't want to go to market.

Ana had become even more weary of life since Memet had gone. Hadn't they all lost a part of themselves when he left? But instead of helping with the extra work, Ana now had her headaches and spent more and more time huddled in the dark corner of her platform.

Mehrigul took a good look at Ana standing there — her eyes dull, her body drooped as if she wanted to descend into the earth. Having the best baked squash at the market would never be reason enough for Ana to go.

She pressed her mother's arm. "Help Ata with the cart. I'm changing into my school skirt," Mehrigul said, and headed for the house. She knew that she herself would never, ever give in to the world Ana had chosen. She'd go to market today and every Wednesday in her skirt, even if it was worn to a rag by the time she got to return to school. Her scarf would be tied in back. Today she'd sell Ana's squash with pride.

* * *

The market was busy. Even before noon, leftover skins from sold squash slices piled high on the cart and spilled over the side to the ground. It pleased Mehrigul to see how customers young and old scraped their teeth along the rind to get the very last taste, threw the rind away, and asked for more. It was Ata who cut the squash. The money collected went into his pocket.

In midafternoon, after the business of the day had peaked, a group of men came to see Ata. They moved a distance from the cart so Mehrigul could not hear what was said, but she could guess. They were probably planning how to get more money to drink and gamble away, or maybe discussing how much money their daughters might be worth if they could send them to work in factories.

One by one, she saw the men glance in the direction of the animal mart, where crowds still lingered among the unsold sheep. They must have spotted a spy, for as quickly as they had come together, they dispersed, blending into the milling crowds.

Her father told her nothing when he returned. Nor did Mehrigul ask. He lifted a squash from the pile, one of the biggest, and cut it into twelve wedges. He ate a piece. "Your ana cooks the best squash," he said, wiping his beard and mustache clean with the back of his hand. "Use the knife to cut up more, if you need to." He picked up his knife and buried it among the uncut squash that lay on the cart. "I'll tell people we have some left and that they'd better come over soon, or it'll be gone."

"Do you have to go now, Ata?" Mehrigul asked, making her voice as calm as possible. Whether he was off to gamble the money in his pocket or to meet with the men again, no good would come of it.

His answer was to walk away. "Remember to buy mutton for Ana," Mehrigul called, hoping some reminder of home would keep him from trouble. Surely he knew the risk.

Her father flipped the back of his hand at her and hurried on.

When she could unclench her teeth, she grabbed a slice of squash and ate it. Wiped her mouth with her hand, wondering why she cared if he got caught.

It surprised her when several women came by for squash. Had Ata been true to his word? The women asked about Ana, and Mehrigul told only how busy she was — with Lali and all.

Another woman appeared. Mehrigul had noticed her lingering about the neighboring carts. Except for her white jacket and fancy scarf, she looked much like the other women, but Mehrigul knew who she was. She was the wife of the local party leader. A Uyghur, no more trusted than her husband.

When Mehrigul was free, the cadre's wife came over and examined the squash as if deciding whether or not to buy a piece. "Your teacher tells me you no longer go to school," she said, still looking at the squash.

Mehrigul kept her head down, too. She couldn't let the woman see the hatred that seethed inside her.

"It's true, isn't it?" The woman moved closer.

"Yes . . . yes," Mehrigul said, struggling for control. *Be calm. Think. Act like Hajinsa — not Ana.* She pulled in a deep breath and lifted her chin. "I'm helping my family for a while — during harvest. I have no intention of giving up my opportunity for an education or my chance to become more proficient in Mandarin. I know that is my key to a successful future." Mehrigul shot her words straight into the face of the cadre's wife.

The woman did not back away. She narrowed her eyes. Looked intently at Mehrigul. Kept looking. Waiting.

A numbness crept inch by inch up Mehrigul's body as she strained to bring in more than tiny gasps of air. She must hold her gaze. She must!

Finally, the cadre's wife backed away. "We'll see, my

dear," she said. A lopsided grin crossed her face. "I'll keep track of you." Her hands rested on her hips as she puffed herself up. "Remember, if you're not in school, it will be easy for me to arrange your papers so you can be sent down south to work in one of the big factories." She shrugged. "We have our quota to fill, you know, and you'll be much more useful to your family if you go."

She paused. The sickening grin left her face. "You're not going to run away like your brother did. Right?"

NINE

ECHOES OF MEMET'S VOICE swirled through Mehrigul's head as she watched the cadre's wife slip back into the bustle of the market.

Don't be taken in, Sister. Don't be taken in. Be careful, Sister, Memet had sung to her just before he left.

Mehrigul shivered at the memory. It had been the end of market day. She and Memet sat on the edge of the cart as they headed home. Not saying much, Memet calling out to the donkey now and then when he went too slow. They'd had a good day, but Memet was on edge, sliding off the cart, jumping on again. "If Ata makes a deal to send you far away to work in a Chinese factory, don't go," he'd said suddenly. "He may try to make you do it. Some of his friends who need money are sending their daughters away. A few of the girls even want to go. But don't, Mehrigul. Just don't do it."

"Why?" Mehrigul had asked.

He wouldn't answer. Wouldn't look at her.

Now he was gone.

Mehrigul had learned the meaning of Memet's warning by listening carefully to the whispered chatter of the women at market. She heard stories of girls who were sent south and never returned. The leaders didn't want their daughters here at home, the women said, where they'd marry Uyghur men and have Uyghur babies. They hoped the girls who were sent away might find Chinese men and marry them; there was a shortage of Han Chinese women. Mehrigul learned it was even worse for the girls who did return home. No Uyghur man would marry one; he couldn't be certain that a girl who'd been sent away was still a virgin.

Don't be taken in, Sister.

Memet had known and now she did, too. And anyone honest with himself knew that things would not change, the Han would never leave.

Mehrigul thought of the courage it had taken for Memet to take a stand against them. They'd tried to kill him, but they would punish her in a different manner. For no offense at all, she'd be sent away. Imprisoned thousands of miles from home. A slave in some factory, helping to make the Han Chinese rich.

Now she'd dared to dream. A dream she might never

have had if the American lady had not seen her basket and liked it. Whether Mrs. Chazen came back or not, even if she had to leave her home for a while, Mehrigul would keep making baskets, her own kind of baskets. She knew a fancy basket was not something a farm woman needed, but somehow she'd reach out to a world beyond a journey in a donkey cart. If she got really good, she'd go to Hotan. Look for Abdul. Maybe he'd help her find a way to sell her baskets. He would know their value.

As Mehrigul stood staring at the place where the cadre's wife had been, another dream crept in. She saw Mrs. Chazen walking away. The three baskets she had carefully wrapped in soft white tissue hung in a bag from the American lady's arm. Three one-hundred-yuan notes lay in Mehrigul's outstretched hands. If she asked Ata for a tiny bit of it to pay her school fees — if he would let her go to school now and then — maybe she could stay home. For a while, anyway.

It was a good dream. The only useful one she had at the moment.

The image of Mrs. Chazen faded.

Mehrigul's hands were empty.

* * *

It was late when Ata came back. If he'd been drinking, it wasn't evident. His face was stern, his jaw set.

"Only a few baskets left. A good day," he said as he passed Mehrigul on his way to retrieve their donkey. Had he looked at her rather than at the cart he might have stopped, sensed something wrong. Or maybe not; Mehrigul wasn't sure how she looked with her brain and body shut down beyond feeling. She couldn't remember moving since she'd watched the cadre's wife walk down the lane and disappear into the crowd.

Now Ata was here. She would not tell him about her visit from the party chief's wife. He'd go right to the cadre and sign whatever he had to, and she'd be on her way to a factory tomorrow.

Mehrigul watched in silence as Ata maneuvered the donkey to the front of the cart, lifted the shafts, tied them to each side of the donkey's collar, then attached the back support.

Automatically, Mehrigul reached to remove the poles that balanced the unhitched cart. She eased herself onto the back of the wagon. The cart tilted as Ata took his place, steering the donkey into the lane with flicks of his willow whip.

"The mutton?" Mehrigul said in little more than a whisper.

Ata reached into his pocket and thrust a wrapped package toward Mehrigul. "You give it to her."

Mehrigul nodded and took the package.

She gathered the coins she'd collected. Presented them to Ata in her open palm, her head lowered. "Yuan. From this afternoon," she said, trying to match the compliant tone her mother had mastered so well.

He took it. Counted it. "You didn't wander off and buy an egg, did you?"

Ata's words changed the numbness she felt to a smoldering fire. He was accusing her of wandering off. Had he been gambling, and was he wondering if she'd seen him? If she'd gone to spy on him?

Mehrigul took a deep breath before she trusted herself to answer. "No, Ata," she said, "though I ate a piece of squash." An edge crept into her voice and she was glad. "I wouldn't have left our cart in the care of the yarn vendor when we were doing such good business."

Ata shrugged. He clicked his tongue at the donkey to make him go faster, and once again seemed interested only in heading home.

They rode in silence. Mehrigul tried to remove from her mind all but the yellow and gold leaves that fell from the poplars that lined the roadway. For a while, anyway, she'd be sweeping leaves into a bag to use as mulch for their fields and food for their donkey. She almost found comfort in that thought.

"You and your mother will be going to market next week. Alone," Ata announced.

Mehrigul let his words hang in the air. She kept her eyes on her feet, which dangled from the back of the wagon, almost touching the ground.

"A man I know is going with the pilgrims to Cow Horn Mountain. I'm going with him to set up a market stall at the foot of the mountain."

She brought her knees to the floor of the cart, turned to face her father. She knew that twice a year Muslim pilgrims from the surrounding countryside made the long trek to the mountain. They prayed at the graves of the Islamic leaders who long ago had won a battle against the Buddhists by smoking them out of their caves. Ata had never gone before. Why now?

Mehrigul stared hard at the back of Ata's head. Even she knew that trip could be dangerous. It wasn't only Uyghur spies who would be there; the Chinese police monitored pilgrimages. If her father got into trouble, they'd lose the farm, everything. Didn't he care anymore?

"You and your mother will have the donkey cart. I'm riding with someone," he said, finally looking at her.

"Ana won't go to market," Mehrigul said.

"She'll have to. You can't go by yourself, and the rest of the squash must be sold."

"What about Lali?" Mehrigul jumped from the cart and walked beside Ata.

He eyed her with disgust. "Take her. It won't hurt her to miss a day of school." He held up his hands, dismissing her. Probably upset he'd bothered to answer.

Mehrigul could think of no other arguments. And, in a way, it was a good thing: If Ata wasn't here, he wouldn't be able to sign papers. She almost smiled when she realized she'd be able to make even more baskets without having to sneak bits of time.

Home was within sight. "I'll run ahead. I can get there faster." Mehrigul bolted, needing to feel the cold wind hit her face.

For the next two weeks she'd think only about making baskets.

TEN

THIS WAS THE SECOND day Mehrigul had been sent to gather walnuts, foraging along the roadway for any that might have been overlooked and had not yet been carried away by rodents. She rode Memet's rusty old bicycle, stopping beside the walnut trees, combing through the fallen leaves.

Two baskets hung from the handlebars. One for Ana; walnuts were rich in nutrition and would help nourish them through the cold. They had always gathered as many as possible. That was their winter treat. The other for Ata, who would take half of what she collected to sell at Cow Horn Mountain.

Mehrigul was reluctant to fill Ata's basket, but that wasn't for her to decide. Ata was unhappy with the small amount she'd gathered the day before. With only two more days before he left, she knew she'd be sent to do even more scavenging, and it wasn't a job she liked. It brought back too many memories of the happy times she and Memet had when they were sent out together to do the gathering, Mehrigul riding on the back of Memet's bicycle. They'd raced to see who could find the most, the winner getting to hide three walnuts in a pocket to eat later.

There was too much aloneness in her life now, and it felt good to see Pati coming toward her on her bicycle as she rounded the last corner before returning home. Pati was waving her arm like a willow bough caught in a sandstorm — weaving across the road, trying to keep her balance. Mehrigul glided to a stop, parked her bicycle, and stood waiting, so pleased that her friend had come to see her and that they'd have a few minutes together.

"Hello!" Pati called in English. She jumped from her bike, leaned it against Mehrigul's, and poured out a stream of words. *"How are you? Today is Saturday. I have come to see you. I am your teacher."*

Mehrigul burst out laughing. *"Hello,* Pati," she answered in English, then switched to Uyghur. "I know that word and not one other of what you just said."

Pati pulled a wrinkled sheet of paper from the school bag slung over her shoulder and fluttered it in front of Mehrigul. "I'm here to teach you English," she said. "I have one hour."

The sun was still high enough in the sky for Mehrigul

to risk a longer absence, though she knew Ata would be growing impatient, more for the return of the bicycle than for her. He'd been riding off on it lately, at any time of day.

"We must move in behind the orchard so no one can see us," Mehrigul said.

They wheeled the bicycles to a clearing near the grape arbor.

"When you see someone," Pati said, "you say *Hello*, or *Hi*. Then you ask how they are. *How are you?* you say."

"*Hi. How are you?*" Mehrigul repeated in English.

"You can ask them how they are right now — that's *today*. Or the day before — that's *yesterday*. Or the day after — and that's *tomorrow*. Now, say after me: *How are you today?*"

"*How are you today?*" Mehrigul said.

Names of the days and the months came next, then numbers from one to ten.

"Pati," Mehrigul said, "this is good. But I'd love to know some special words." She stood. Unthinking, she twined a narrow stem that hung from the grapevines around her finger, pulling it, testing it for strength and size. *You can test a vine*, she thought, *but how do you test a friend, to know if she can really keep a secret?* She'd trusted Memet. He'd been a good secret keeper. He might laugh when she said something silly, but he never told.

She'd shared many things with Pati but never anything of such importance. She needed so much to have someone to talk to now. Someone to tell why she wanted to learn English.

"Come with me, Pati," Mehrigul said. "I have something to show you in the bamboo patch."

They walked along the road to the grove. Mehrigul carefully chose a new entryway into the thicket so that no clear path would lead to her special hiding place. Memet had taught her that.

She and Pati pushed through the culms to the spot where Mehrigul had stored her piles of cut grapevines and her baskets. Three new baskets lay on the ground, sheltered by cut branches. She removed the covering. There was one cone-shaped basket. Another was unlike any basket Mehrigul had ever seen. She had cut vine pieces as long as the distance from her thumb to her little finger when she stretched her hand wide. Instead of weaving, she had laid out seven pieces side by side, separating them so they formed a square. She had laced two vine pieces across the ends of this base, then two more across the ends of these, building row by row until the basket was shaped like a square box. That had looked too plain, so Mehrigul had added handles of twisted, curved vines, creating graceful arches on two sides.

The one she picked up was a ribbed basket shaped like half of a watermelon, with vine ribs hanging from a thick, oblong hoop, linked together with a simple in-and-out weave. She faced Pati with this basket cradled in her arms. She squinted to better see her friend's reaction in the muted light of the grove.

She saw the smile she'd hoped for.

"They're beautiful," Pati said.

Then Mehrigul saw Pati suck in her breath, as if trying to keep from saying something.

"What, Pati? Tell me."

"They're different from your chong ata's." Pati reached for the square basket with the arched handles. Turned it around in her hands. "It's great to look at, but it won't hold much. And that one?" She pointed to the basket Mehrigul was holding. "It looks like you've woven cornhusks or something into it."

"I have," Mehrigul said, her voice quiet and composed. "You see, I'm not certain my baskets have any real use. But Pati . . ." She stopped. "I want you to keep a secret."

"Sure," Pati said.

"I mean a real secret, one you must tell no one."

"I'm your friend. Of course I will."

"You must keep your word."

"Mehrigul, I promise."

"A lady from America saw the old basket I'd hung on the donkey cart and bought it. She asked me to make others. She'll come back to the market a week from Wednesday . . . to buy more. That's why I want to learn English."

Pati swung her shoulders left to right, back and forth, in what Mehrigul knew to be her greatest show of delight.

"That's exciting," Pati said. Then again there was a question in her eyes. "Has your grandfather seen your baskets?"

"Not yet. I'm waiting until Ata goes on pilgrimage, then I'll bring them for him to see. He must be the first one in the family to see them," Mehrigul said. "It will be important that he likes them."

Pati shrugged. "He might think using cornhusks is too common for an American lady."

"But look." Mehrigul held out her basket. "Don't you think they add texture and color?" A grin suddenly crossed her face. "If you just happen to see a certain young man tomorrow, and he just happens to have leftover scraps of red or blue felt, I'd be very glad to weave them into my baskets. You're right, a lady from America might like that better."

"I'll try to make it happen," Pati said.

Mehrigul placed her baskets on the ground and covered them again with the fallen bamboo culms.

"I wish I knew the English word for 'basket,'" she said.

Pati folded her hands across her waist. This was another sign Mehrigul knew — her friend had something she was reluctant to say.

"Oh, all right," Pati said finally, digging into her bag and pulling out a small book. "You need this more than I do. It gives the English word for the same word in Mandarin. The teacher let me have it. I was going to be the smart one and teach you, but you can borrow it." She handed the battered book to Mehrigul. "You need more words than I can teach you right away."

Mehrigul made a low bow in acceptance, then quickly opened the book.

"*Lanzi* is the Mandarin word." Mehrigul searched through the *l*'s. "Here it is," she said. "The word is *basket. Basket*," she repeated. "*Basket.*"

Pati stood tall. "So you say to the American lady, *Do you like basket?*"

Swaying and singing, *"Do you like basket? Do you like basket?"*, they made their way back through the bamboo onto the road. A lightness swept through Mehrigul, lifting some of her doubts, her fears that the meeting with Mrs. Chazen had been so outside her real world that it could only have been imagined.

But Ata coming toward them, seeing them emerge from the bamboo, was more real than she wished. "What were you doing in there?" he asked, angling his head and frowning.

Mehrigul had no answer. She froze the carefree look of a moment ago on her face to hide the guilt she felt about her baskets.

The growing silence spoke of secrets.

Pati took a step toward Ata. "We heard a strange birdcall," she said in a sweet, innocent voice. "We rushed through the bamboo, hoping to get a glimpse." She laughed. "I guess we were just having fun, for we surely would have scared it away."

Ata tightened his lips. "Uhmm," he mumbled, not bothering to acknowledge Pati. His attention was drawn to the book Mehrigul held in her hand. "What's that?" he said.

"A school book Pati brought me, so I can study."

Mehrigul kept her voice strong and even, but she couldn't control the trembling in her hands. She clutched her arms and the book to her, hoping Ata wouldn't notice. "The bicycle is by the grapevines. I'll bring it home right away."

"No. You'll bring it to me now, and you will walk home." Ata's voice was quiet. He stood with his hands on his waist, just looking at her. He raised his eyebrows, but not in anger — that would be easy to recognize. If he thought they'd lied to him, why wasn't he shouting?

Mehrigul felt Pati's arm around her, hurrying her away toward their parked bicycles.

ELEVEN

MEHRIGUL TOOK ONE LAST look at the road before she passed the corner of the house that would obscure her view. She hadn't planned to show Chong Ata her baskets today, but for the first time in long memory she and her grandfather were alone. Ana's headaches had gotten so bad that she couldn't leave her bed. Ata was driving her to the doctor in the cotton township. Ana had known the village healer since childhood. He was the only one she'd allow to take her pulse and check for symptoms, to prepare herbs for her to brew into a tea. Ata insisted Ana see him before he left on pilgrimage.

Mehrigul took the risk that they might change their minds and return early. She wanted so badly to know if Chong Ata thought her baskets worthy of showing to the American lady.

"I've brought two of my baskets for you to see, Chong Ata," Mehrigul said. She squatted next to him in the yard where he was at work, surrounded by his willow branches. "I need to know if you like them."

As Chong Ata reached forward to place his work on the ground, the front panel of his coat flapped open, revealing the sheepskin lining with its long, shaggy strands of wool. Was he already so cold he had to wear it? He would sleep inside when the winter winds came, join the family on the wooden sleeping platforms they shared in the room that was for cooking and eating, for living and sleeping. Still, they never had enough blankets to guard them from the cold that penetrated the cracks in their walls of poplar sticks and mud. They had no money to buy a proper stove with pipes leading under the sleeping platforms to heat them. Heat from pipes was a marvel she knew from visiting Pati. Pati's beloved grandmother, her whole family had this comfort.

Shouldn't she be out collecting their winter store of fallen branches and twigs for the brazier rather than making baskets? Who would do that if she were sent away? The baskets in her arms grew heavy with her guilt. Her use of time to make them was a luxury. How many more days of absence from school would the cadre and his wife allow before Mehrigul was picked to fill their quota of factory workers?

They hadn't come after her yet. And if she made even more baskets — and was paid a hundred yuan each! — maybe her family could even buy some coal. That would keep Chong Ata warmer than any twigs.

Chong Ata cleared his throat, his hands idle, waiting.

"I'm sorry," Mehrigul said. "Maybe I'm afraid to show you my baskets, for fear you won't like them."

Chong Ata said nothing. He closed his eyes and held out his hands. Mehrigul handed him her square basket. She watched as he traced the arches of the handles with his fingers. He held the basket between his hands, as if measuring the length of each side. He felt the bottom, tested the bindings. Then opened his cloudy eyes, squinting to bring an image into place.

A shiver ran through Mehrigul's body. His expression told nothing. There was no scowl, no smile. He looked at the basket for the longest time.

"Mehrigul." He finally spoke, calling her not Granddaughter, as he always did, but by her name. Was this a sign of Chong Ata's new respect for her?

"I'm proud that you have created a different kind of basket," he said. "One I have never seen before. I believe the lady at the market will like it. It's sturdy and well made." He handed the basket back to Mehrigul, all the time nodding approval.

Still she shivered, but this time from relief. "Thank you, Chong Ata," she said. "I have another for you to see."

As she reached for the ribbed basket, her hands froze. Not that she'd heard anything. It was a feeling—not a sound. "I'll be right back." She sprang up, darted to the corner of the house. Her eyes searched the roadway. No donkey carts were in sight. She'd sensed her own fear.

When her heart stopped pounding, she went back to Chong Ata's side. "Please don't tell Ata you've seen my baskets," she said. "He thought the basket I sold was worthless and doesn't want me to make more. He'd say they're worth nothing more than to feed to a goat."

Chong Ata's body curved into a ball of sadness.

"It may be hard for your father to see beauty in anything these days," he said. "You must try to forgive him. We are all grieving from the shadow that has been cast over our lives." He rocked his body back and forth, letting his head drop onto his chest.

Mehrigul tightened her hold on the ribbed basket. Forgiveness of Ata was not something that came easily to her heart. If Chong Ata knew, if he'd caught Ata gambling, would he say to forgive him? Weren't they all grieving from more shadows than she could think of?

Air seemed to flow into Chong Ata's body again. He looked up, gave a long sigh.

"I believe you have another basket to show me," he said.

Mehrigul eased her grasp on the basket and placed it in his outstretched hands. She would not let this rare — maybe her last — private moment with Chong Ata be spoiled with thoughts of Ata.

She watched as he again closed his eyes, explored her work with his hands. Chong Ata's white mustache curved around a broad smile as he fingered the cornhusks interwoven with the vines.

"For many years now," he said, "I have made only baskets for daily use." His eyes open again, he held the basket close to his face. "You have made something that is uncommon."

"Do you think the American lady will like it?" Mehrigul moved closer to Chong Ata, examining the basket herself, trying to see it as if for the first time.

"I believe she saw a particular quality in the basket she bought. Something she liked. And wished to have more." Chong Ata lowered the basket, cradling it in his lap. "Baskets don't have to all be alike. Cotton can be woven into plain cloth. If you change the pattern of the warp and the weft you get a different weave. If the threads are dyed you get different colors."

All of a sudden Chong Ata leaned his head back, shaking it, almost losing his big, black wooly hat. "Why, we cover the mud walls of our homes with bright, colorful cloth full of flowers and patterns," he said. "That tells something about the nature of our Uyghur hearts."

Chong Ata picked up Mehrigul's ribbed basket that still lay in his lap and held it out to her. "Our people should never lose the joy of making beautiful things with their hands — especially when so much else is being taken away from us." He paused. Looked away, into the distance. "I know no reason at all why a basket has to be plain."

"Thank you, Chong Ata," Mehrigul said.

He gathered the willow spokes that lay at his feet and began again to weave. "Your father wants some of my baskets to take on pilgrimage. I must not be idle."

"Nor must I." Mehrigul gathered her baskets. "I'll store mine. I have a special place. I'll be right back."

She slid cautiously around the corner of the house. The way was clear. She ran down the road toward the stand of bamboo, stirring up dust and dirt from the roadway and not caring.

If only Chong Ata is right, she thought. *That someone might like a basket just because it's different. The American lady wouldn't be coming back if she didn't want more.*

If she comes back.

Minutes later, Mehrigul was in Chong Ata's workroom, removing the branches she needed from the bag of cut willow he kept there. The moistened branches had already turned from yellow to deep tan, a color that was Mehrigul's favorite. She brought the branches close to her nose and drew in the sweet scent. It was Chong Ata's smell — the smell of his newly made baskets — that always brought contentment.

"I'm going to help you, Chong Ata. You'll need to make one less basket today," Mehrigul said as she settled next to him. "Then, when Lali comes home, we'll go inside and have tea."

"Perhaps," he said. "Your father leaves tomorrow. It's important to make as many baskets as I can." He reached into his pocket and pulled out his Yengisar knife. He laid it between them.

A wave of emotion swept through Mehrigul. She'd helped Chong Ata countless times. He'd taught her how to weave, bind the rims, lash on handles. Was the knife between them his way of saying she'd earned a full place at his side? She would keep the memory of this moment with her, no matter where she was.

Mehrigul found comfort in arranging the long, thin willow branches in front of her like the spokes of a wheel. With a weaver in her hand she worked around the center to build the base. Willow was easier to maneuver than rough grapevines.

Chong Ata was working on the sides of his basket, holding the spokes upward with his feet as he pushed and pulled his weaver in front of two spokes, then behind one, in front of two, then behind. He began to hum. Mehrigul heard no melody in the sound, only a pattern of rhythms, repeated over and over again as his fingers worked in and out and around the basket.

Mehrigul began to hum, too, keeping most of the sound inside her. But somehow Chong Ata knew, in spite of his dull hearing. He stopped working and reached to pat her hand. Then, again, their fingers returned to work. Their voices joined. Two over, one under, two over, one under . . .

TWELVE

It was late morning when Mehrigul heard the rumble of a truck coming down the road — the sound Ata had been listening for since daybreak. Ata hurried to the road, waving so the driver would know he'd found their home.

A screech of brakes ruptured the air as the truck shuddered to a standstill. Everything about the dusty, broken-down thing conveyed hopelessness to Mehrigul. How could such a wreck, with its taped-on headlights, ever reach Cow Horn Mountain? They might better have driven half a day in their donkey carts to get there.

Mehrigul watched a large, burly man get out of the passenger side of the cab and walk to the driver's side. He untied the rope that held the door shut, and the driver, a strapping young man, got out. Where would Ata sit? There was no room for him in the cab. Or in the truck bed, piled with crates and bags. Shoved into a corner were a black sheep and two black lambs. A young man stood beside them.

Would Ata agree to ride in back with the animals?

What if he didn't go? She'd counted on the time to make more baskets.

Mehrigul's concern was forgotten when the two men from the cab walked into the yard, toward Chong Ata, who squatted there in his bare feet, working to finish another basket before Ata left. She rushed to her grandfather. "The men going on pilgrimage with Ata are coming to pay their respects, Chong Ata. Let me help you up," she said.

Guilt washed over her. Why hadn't she thought to get him ready? Why hadn't Ata? Guests always paid homage to her grandfather. It was Ana who would have remembered he needed a clean shirt, reminded him to wear shoes when visitors were expected. Today she was resting. She would not see Ata off, nor had she helped in the preparations.

Still, there was dignity in the way Chong Ata rose, his eyes old and soft above his almost pure-white beard.

The thickset older man reached Chong Ata first. *"As-salam alaykum,"* he said. "Peace be unto you." His right hand rose to his chest, palm open. He gave a slight bow.

Chong Ata offered the same gesture. *"Wa alaykum as-salam.* And unto you peace," he said, his gaze steady.

The driver, the younger man, repeated the greeting and the raising of his hand, as did Chong Ata.

"This is Osman . . . and his son," Ata said, his voice curt and jarring after the gentleness of the greetings that had just taken place. "His other son is in the truck, tending the sheep they'll deliver on the way to the mountain."

As Ata introduced the men to Chong Ata, he stepped in front of Mehrigul, excluding her.

Anger flooded through Mehrigul, and she inched backwards. His rudeness embarrassed her. The bitterness in his voice stung. Was he slighting her because Memet was not there — had left Ata without a son at his side? Or to remind her of her place? A thankless girl he'd had to feed and raise, who'd then go off and marry and work in someone else's household.

Should Mehrigul dissolve into the earth because she'd not been born a boy?

She slipped away and watched unobserved from the doorway. It pleased her to hear the words of respect Osman spoke to her chong ata, to see the regard he held for his elder cross his rough, leathered face. He seemed to know that her grandfather carried with him the history of the Uyghur's struggles in this unforgiving oasis. That he was in the presence of someone who knew both the pride and the hardships of his people.

"Mehrigul," Ata called, his strident tone reminding her she was far from special. "Bring the goods in the house to the truck."

"Yes, Ata," she said, in as cold a voice as she could find within her. She went to the kitchen to gather the bags she'd filled with walnuts and dried peaches from their precious store, the bag of naan she'd baked, and the raisins that Ata would take to eat on his journey.

When Mehrigul emerged from the house, she collided with Ata, coming from Chong Ata's workroom. Two bags were slung over his shoulder. She'd packed all the baskets into one bag. Why had he repacked them?

"What are you staring at?" Ata shot the words at Mehrigul as he shoved her out of the way with his elbow.

Mehrigul stumbled backwards, struggling to keep a hold on the heavy bags she carried. Why was he being so hurtful to her? Whatever she'd done, Mehrigul would take care not to anger him further. She headed for the truck, feeling oddly comforted by the presence of strangers.

Osman took the bags from her. He gave no greeting. If Ata hadn't acknowledged her as a beloved daughter, surely he had no obligation.

After Ata placed his bags in the truck bed, everything

was fastened down. Both of Osman's sons now crouched next to the bleating sheep. Ata tied Osman's door on the driver's side and took the passenger seat.

They drove away.

There was no wave goodbye or instructions to take good care of Ana. No warnings about being lazy. No reminders to do chores on time.

Chong Ata was still beside the house when Mehrigul returned from the road. He held out his open palms as Mehrigul approached. She laid her hands in his, and the strength and comfort of his gnarled fingers began to calm her.

"I think my father was overcome with sorrow to see a man with two sons. Don't you, Chong Ata? That Memet was not here beside him was more than he could bear. Wasn't it?" She squeezed Chong Ata's hands. "Do you think that's why he acted so strangely toward me, that it's really Memet who has angered him?"

Chong Ata's eyes were so moist with caring, she thought her heart would break open. "There is no excuse for his behavior toward you, my beautiful Mehrigul."

THIRTEEN

Move faster, Lali. I know it's early, but you're the only help I have. *Kwai dian.* Quickly," Mehrigul said in Mandarin, trying to sound like a teacher so her sleepy sister would liven up and be useful. The donkey cart was only half loaded and it was already time to go. There'd be no good spots left at market if they didn't leave soon. Mehrigul shooed Lali ahead of her into the house, filled their bags with more squash, and returned to the cart.

It had been long past the setting of the sun when Mehrigul decided she couldn't bake another squash. She'd worked every minute since Ata left and still a few squash would have to be sold unbaked. Ana would be disappointed, but Mehrigul had insisted she not help. It was enough that she was going to market.

Mehrigul went now to wake her. It was unusual for Ana to sleep so late, but the teas the doctor had provided did seem to bring her rest and comfort.

"Time to get up, Ana," she said, shaking her arm. "We need to leave."

The peace of Ana's dreaming vanished as she sat upright. "Yes, I'll go . . . I know I must. Why didn't you call me earlier? I should be helping," she said, and now she was standing, pulling her skirt from the clothesline above the sleeping platform.

"Wear your red sweater today," Mehrigul said. "For happiness."

Ana's hands folded in front of her, that horrible gesture of resignation as she began to withdraw into her cocoon.

Mehrigul took Ana's hands in hers, placed them at her sides. "I'll bring your sweater," she said, heading toward the wooden chest where it was stored. "After you eat, I'll braid your hair."

Ana's eyes rose to meet hers, and for the first time in many weeks Mehrigul thought her mother had actually seen her.

So little was going right this morning. How many times had Mehrigul watched Memet and Ata harness their donkey? The animal would just stand there, accepting the collar, the harnesses, the belly straps. Not for Mehrigul. He kept striking out with his front hoof, nipping at her with his foul-smelling teeth, as if to tell her she was doing it wrong. "Hold still!" she shouted, and he brayed so loudly she thought every donkey within three kilometers would come to his rescue. She tried gentler urgings and finally got everything on him that was needed. She was glad this had happened out of Chong Ata's sight. He would have insisted it was his job, and it was not wise for him to do so strenuous a task.

Ana and Lali were by the cart when Mehrigul led the donkey from the shed. They helped shove the shafts of the cart through the loops of the belly band and into the loops in the collar. Ana held the donkey while Mehrigul ran back to Chong Ata's room, where he was already busy sorting and soaking willow branches for his day's work.

"We'll return as soon as possible ... when all the squash is sold," she said. He nodded, kept on working. Perhaps only Mehrigul worried about his being left alone. "Take time for tea, Chong Ata."

"Yes, yes," he said. "Go on. Get started before the sun climbs any higher." He reached out, picked up a branch that had fallen from the pile, and flicked it with a dismissive gesture, as if to tell her it was all right to go.

There was still a bite in the air as they made their way along the narrow, poplar-lined roadway. The old donkey went at his own pace and Mehrigul saw little reason to interfere since he ignored all the commands she called to him and seemed to hardly notice when she used the whip. They passed sheep grazing at roadside, a woman carrying buckets of water hanging from a pole slung over her back.

But it was far from quiet. Lali's chatter was loud enough to drown out the high-pitched twitter of the wagtail birds. She'd been allowed to wear her red jacket, plaid skirt, red leggings, and white strap shoes even though she wasn't going to school. Ana pulled Lali close to her side, their legs and feet twining and untwining as they dangled from the side of the cart. Lali told stories of her friends. She sent her childhood songs into the air in a sweet, high voice. Ana and sometimes Mehrigul joined in.

The roadway became crowded as they neared the market, a steady stream of carts joining them. Mehrigul got down to lead the donkey. The sand and dirt stirred by her feet added a new layer of grime to her shoes and baggy pants. In spite of her good resolution, she hadn't taken time to change to her skirt. And none of that mattered. There had been a rare moment of contentment for the three of them this morning that lingered in her heart.

Lali's songs got louder as more noise surrounded them. She began to sing in Mandarin, a song she'd learned in school. Mehrigul caught her eye and she stopped. Put her hand over her mouth. Lali was almost always good about remembering their rule. But Ana had heard, and Mehrigul supposed it was enough to remind her that Lali was part of the outside world — where Ana no longer belonged. Her mother quietly folded her hands in her lap.

The spot next to the wool seller was taken. Mehrigul led the donkey deeper into the market, searching for a place where lots of people would come by and be tempted to give their bellies a treat when they saw the rich orange meat of the baked squash and got a sniff of its oniony smell. What they earned today would be the only yuan they could count on this week. Ata would likely spend more on his trip than he'd take in. Mehrigul gave the donkey a hard yank as she pulled him into an empty space.

The woman next to them had her cart piled high with potatoes and green and red peppers. She was already balancing her scale, weighing a few peppers for a customer. She seemed friendly enough, from all Mehrigul could tell. It was mostly her eyes and wrinkled forehead that showed under the yellow and red scarf she'd draped around her head. Ana had returned her greeting and appeared to be managing well when Mehrigul left to tether the donkey to a tree at the edge of the market.

It was Mehrigul who was not at ease. She searched the crowds for any sign of the cadre's wife as she hurried back to the cart. The woman seemed to do her dealings in private. Mehrigul's best protection was to be surrounded by a crowd of people.

By late morning brisk business was being done along the row of carts. Mehrigul had chosen their spot wisely. She'd not seen the party chief or his wife lurking anywhere nearby, and Ana's squash was selling well.

Lali was their salesman. "My ana's squash is the best you'll find," she sang out. Then, when she'd lured a customer over, she whispered, "She has a secret recipe." She seemed to know when she could take someone by the arm and bring him or her to the cart, where Mehrigul would slice a piece and haggle for the yuan. Ana sat in back on an overturned crate.

Mehrigul was bringing more uncut squash to the cart bed when she saw the cadre's wife approach the vegetable seller and pick out a few peppers. As her purchase was being weighed, she looked over and caught Mehrigul watching her. For an awful moment their eyes locked. With no change of expression on her face, the cadre's wife took her bag of peppers and walked away.

She had found out what she needed to know. Mehrigul was not in school.

Business slowed by midafternoon. Mehrigul wanted to leave, for the crowds were thinning. She dreaded the thought that the cadre's wife might come back. But there were still two squash to sell. Mehrigul lowered the price. Lali had tired of playing seller, and most of their customers were people who came by for potatoes and peppers.

Half a squash was still left when Mehrigul spotted Pati on the path by the yarn seller, where she might expect Mehrigul to be. Mehrigul stepped into the lane and waved her arms, delighted to see her friend, until she saw Hajinsa with her, her red high-platform shoes gliding over the dusty ground.

Mehrigul dropped her arms, but she'd been seen. Seen in her wrinkled and dirty peach-colored pants, her soiled shirt, her scarf tied under her chin. She pulled Lali in front of her, hoping her sister's pretty red jacket and pure white scarf would be a shield.

"Pati! Pati!" Lali called, running to throw her arms

around her sister's friend. Leaving Mehrigul, in all her humiliation, to watch them come arm in arm to the cart. Hajinsa shrugged and followed, a scowl on her face.

Mehrigul pivoted and went to Ana. Brought her from the back of the cart.

"It's so nice to see you," Pati said, and then Ana's red sweater and Pati's bright red jacket with the white buttons came together in a hug. Ana and Mehrigul had not touched their faces together in a hug for many weeks, many months . . . maybe longer.

Ana smiled. There was too much red, too much happiness, for Mehrigul. She wanted only to earn a few more yuan and go home.

A cheery "Hi" came from behind her. She turned to see Lali clutching Hajinsa, guiding her toward the cart, looking up at her as if she'd discovered an empress.

Mehrigul erased all emotion from her face and went to Lali. She placed her hands on her sister's shoulders and squeezed. Lali got the message, and whatever chatter might have come next broke off. She leaned back against Mehrigul.

"I would like you to meet my ana," Mehrigul said, stepping aside with Lali so Ana and Hajinsa faced each other.

"*Tinchliqmu?* At peace?" Ana greeted Hajinsa in the traditional Uyghur way, her manner hesitant but polite.

"*Tinchliq! Siz-chu?* At peace! And you?"

Hajinsa had answered with the right words, but Ana's eyes flickered, then lowered. "*Tinchliq,*" she said, finishing the greeting, her voice barely audible.

Was it the way Hajinsa stood, her cocked head, her cold voice? She'd let Ana know in her greeting that Ana was as much a peasant as her daughter.

"I'm going to take Mehrigul away for a moment," Pati said, taking Ana's hand in hers in a kindly gesture. "I'll send her right back, I promise."

Mehrigul shooed Lali in Ana's direction and followed Pati and Hajinsa a short distance. She'd seen a bag hanging from Pati's arm and hoped it held felt pieces that might decorate her baskets. She wouldn't let Hajinsa's disrespect stop her from getting what she wanted.

"*How are you doing?*" Pati asked, speaking English, and that, too, added to Mehrigul's discomfort. She'd not had time to study English since Pati's visit.

"*We have a great English teacher,*" Hajinsa said. "*She is getting CDs for me so I can study on my own.*" She rattled on in English that had no meaning for Mehrigul but was surely meant to make her feel inferior.

"Ah . . . about what I promised. Remember?" Pati interrupted, speaking now in Mandarin.

Were they no longer to speak Uyghur? Was that only a language for poor farmers? Every inch of Mehrigul wanted to stomp away, but not as much as she wanted what might be in Pati's bag.

She forced a pleasant expression. "Of course I remember," Mehrigul answered in Uyghur. She couldn't help but notice, though, that Hajinsa crossed her hands behind her head and rolled her eyes. Then shrugged again in her infuriating way as Pati slipped the bag from her arm and handed it to Mehrigul.

"Can we go, Pati? Is your errand done?" Hajinsa said. "If you want me to show you where to buy leggings with lace trim, we have to leave now. I can't keep my ana waiting."

Pati nodded. Her eyes made quick contact with Mehrigul's before she turned and followed Hajinsa into the maze of the marketplace, but Mehrigul didn't know what the gaze meant. What she did know was that her best friend had moved on and was walking, if not arm in arm, at least side by side with someone Mehrigul did not like or trust, into a world that was out of her reach.

Not even Lali's songs comforted Mehrigul as their old

donkey pulled them toward home. So what if she were sent away? Would that be much worse, Mehrigul wondered, than the life she must resign herself to here? How long before she'd become like Ana and need her teas to get through the day? She couldn't imagine leaving Lali and Chong Ata, but might they be better off without her? If she sent money home?

Suppose Ata did let her keep a little of the money from selling her baskets to pay school fees and allowed her to return to school for a handful of days. Then what? Come spring, there would again be much to do on the farm. More than Ata could ever do alone, even if he labored full-time.

Mehrigul saw no future for herself whether she stayed or went.

FOURTEEN

At first it was a low, moaning sound. Maybe Ana releasing some pent-up sorrow in her herb-induced sleep. Mehrigul burrowed deeper into her pallet, liking the warmth and the thoughts that filled her head. In a short time she'd get up, borrow Chong Ata's knife, and head for the grapevine patch. Free at last from fear that Ata would find her. There were chores, but today she'd declared a holiday. She'd do nothing but make more baskets, fancier ones woven with the strips of blue and red felt Pati had given her. She had less than a week.

The moans grew louder. Howling. Whistling now. From outside.

Mehrigul sat up, trying to understand. Sounds like hundreds of beating drums pounded the roof, the mud walls.

She rushed to the door. Struggled to keep it from flying open as she peeked out into a wall of swirling sand and dust. Coughing, choking as the fine grains invaded her nostrils and throat, stung her eyes. She forced the door closed and stood numb to the reality of what was happening.

The gods of the Taklamakan Desert had chosen this day to send their winds and sands over the oasis.

She spat sand and grit into her hand and blinked sand from her eyes.

Then she heard a crash. Their roof ladder hitting the ground. What else was being blown away? Who'd take care of it? Try to stop it? Ata? Memet?

Chong Ata! Mehrigul grabbed her clothes. She must help him inside before he tried to do it on his own.

Lali's whimpering drew her to their platform. "What's happening, Mehrigul?"

Mehrigul tucked her sister back under the bedcover. "The desert dunes are paying a visit. Reminding us we're neighbors." She brushed Lali's forehead with a kiss before bringing the blanket over her head. "You're safe, though. I won't let the sand inside, only the bit that sneaks through the cracks. Go back to sleep. It's still early," she said.

"I need to go to school."

"Not today. I'm bringing Chong Ata in. Your job is to make sure he stays. He'll want to help outside. But he can't, Lali. It's dangerous for him. Get Ana to help. Do you understand?"

"I do," Lali whispered, already sitting upright, her eyes wide open.

Mehrigul put on an extra sweater, then wrapped a silk scarf, the most tightly woven one they had, over her nose and mouth, tying it in back. She wound another scarf around her forehead, half shielding her eyes, covering her hair.

Mehrigul slipped out the door into the opaque landscape, keeping her body skintight to the wall as she inched toward the door to Chong Ata's workroom.

Even in the darkness of the room she could see her grandfather huddled against the wall.

"You must be with us, Chong Ata," she shouted, hoping he could hear her through the noise of the storm.

"There is much we must do," he said as Mehrigul went to his side and helped him to stand.

"Not now," Mehrigul said. "Hold the rug over your face. I'll lead you."

They crept back the short distance along the wall to the main door, Mehrigul feeling her grandfather's reluctance to follow her. She knew how much he wished he could help.

Lali was waiting inside. "Get the broom, Lali. Sweep the sand from Chong Ata's coat."

Mehrigul looked at Ana, who stood motionless beside

the kitchen platform. "Don't just stand there, Ana. Please help. Do we need twigs? Water? Check for me. I'm going back out."

"Twigs," Ana answered, turning her head away. "I'm sorry, Mehrigul. I'm trying to wake up. I know what is happening."

"Look after Lali. That you can do." Lali was standing with the broom in her hand, looking as frightened as a lost chick. Mehrigul could offer no comfort to Lali, or Ana, or to herself. She had no idea what she should be doing.

"Just stay in the house. Don't let anyone follow me," she said, nodding her head toward Chong Ata as she thrust the door open against the storm.

Again, Mehrigul stuck close to the side of the house as she went to look at their ladder. Its top rungs had smashed against a pile of stones, but it was worth saving.

She grabbed hold and began dragging it toward the shed. A sudden gust whipped at her as she rounded the corner of the house. She lay low to the ground, clutching the ladder, studying the storm, the direction of the wind. And through the narrow slits of her eyelids she saw streaks of yellow flying through the thick, gray air. Their dried corncobs, lifted from their rooftop storage by the wind and carried away over the yard, to the fields and beyond.

Airborne kernels of food that were meant for their winter soups, cobs that might have fueled their fires. Gone.

Were the peaches flying, too? Or swept into a corner, covered with so much sand and dirt they could never be eaten?

The ruined food was all she could think of as she crawled, dragging the ladder, across the open stretch to the shed.

It was her fault. Why hadn't she read the signs of a coming storm the night before? Ata and Memet would have. Their food could have been saved.

She knew why. She'd been caught up in her selfishness. What was more important than a good night's sleep so she could rise early and finally get to her baskets? Her mind had been filled with visions of the new things she'd make — baskets with colorful red and blue strips of felt woven into the design. Not once had she listened for a change of sound in the wind, a distant stirring. Nor had she watched the patterns of the birds; they knew to fly toward the mountains, away from the approaching desert storm. The leaves on the willow trees would have been slanting upward, if she had only looked.

Chong Ata should have known! Mehrigul stopped the thought. Let the pelting of sand against her face be punishment. Chong Ata could barely hear or see. It was not for him to have known. Nor Ana. She, herself, had given Ana a cup of the doctor's soothing tea.

The blame was Mehrigul's. And it compounded by the minute. The donkey was kicking at the shed, braying, trying to break loose. Mehrigul gave a final heave to the ladder, left it under the cart, and rushed to find an old feed bag. Dodging nips and kicks, she pulled it over the donkey's head and tied it. At least the worst of the sand would be kept from his eyes and nose.

She found rope and lashed the donkey cart and ladder to a storm-bent poplar that stood beside the shed. There was nothing else to do. The pile of hay for the donkey had already been carried away. When the storm ended, he'd have to eat the sand-filled straw that had blown into a corner.

For a moment, Mehrigul rested against the open lattice of the shed, resisting the urge to rub her eyes, to take in more than shallow breaths. Around her the sky, the ground, were a colorless blend of hurtling sand. Her world stopped a few meters from where she pressed against the wooden planks. Thoughts of other chores — things she should have done the night before — were of no help now.

She picked up the pitiful handful of twigs trapped at

the edge of the shed and began to fight her way back to the house.

Lali ran to her when she came inside. "Wait," Mehrigul said. She dropped the kindling, signaled with her hands. Lali stopped short, her eyes wide at the sight of her ghost-like sister.

"Bring me my other pants, Lali. Okay?" Mehrigul said as she began to shed her sand-filled garments.

As she reached to untie the scarves, she was surprised to find Ana at her side. "Close your eyes," Ana said, helping Mehrigul remove the wrappings. "You must not let any more sand get into your eyes or nose."

Mehrigul felt a damp cloth wipe over her eyelids, her eyebrows, her forehead, Ana's gentle strokes cleaning away the film of dust and sand that had come in through the narrow slit between the scarves. "Thank you, Ana," Mehrigul said.

"Change, then come have tea," Ana said.

Even after she removed her outer sweater and put on her other pants, sand pricked every inch of Mehrigul's body as she moved to the eating cloth. She welcomed Ana's caring and the chance to sit while Ana built the fire and brewed tea. Then, suddenly, Ana was behind her with the tea bowl. The smell of sulfur hit her nostrils for the first time as she reached to take the bowl from her mother's hands. Ana had used precious bits of coal from their reserve to build a fire.

For a while Chong Ata, Ana, Lali, and Mehrigul sat in silence, drinking tea and eating stale naan from the tin Ana placed in the middle of the cloth. The only sound was that of the shifting sands pummeling their home.

Ana finally spoke. "Our food . . . on the roof . . ." Her voice told Mehrigul that her mother knew the truth.

"Blown away. Ruined, I suppose." Mehrigul heard her own voice, weak and pitiful. Her eyes stung and watered. Her mouth tasted like dirt. She had no more to say that would not be mean and hurtful. Feeling angry at Ata, and Memet, too, for not being here, seemed as useless as blaming the desert. She crawled to the side of the sleeping platform, leaned her head against the wooden frame.

"Mehrigul," Chong Ata said. He was beside her. "It's rare to have a storm in November. They are expected in the spring, not now. Let us rest. When the wind calms we will know the damage." He put his hand over hers. "Our people have chosen this land. We have learned to survive."

Chong Ata went back to the eating cloth, once again turning into a tiny ball. His eyes were closed, his lips moving. She thought he might be praying. Lali had crawled onto Ana's lap, finding comfort. Mehrigul closed her eyes. It helped to take away the sting.

"Come, look. It's a miracle!" Lali cried, jumping up and down, then racing out the door.

Mehrigul's eyes were sticky. Crusted shut. She rubbed them gently as she rose and headed for the door.

It *was* a miracle. Rain! After hours of sand, rain had come. They had no more than two or three days of rain in a year — a little over one centimeter in all, if they were lucky. And today it was raining!

Mehrigul walked outside. She lifted her face to the gentle drops, letting the rain restore her body as it would restore the air and the land — if only it would last long enough to penetrate the hard-packed earth.

Lali grabbed her hands. "Dance, Mehrigul. Dance." She pulled Mehrigul round and round until they were twirling and stomping like a pair of featherheads.

Ana and Chong Ata stood in the rain, too. Maybe, Mehrigul thought, this was what Chong Ata had been praying for, and Allah had answered his prayer. Chong Ata still had on his sheepskin hat, but his face was raised to the rain.

The donkey brayed, perhaps not so much from joy as

from hunger. "Okay, Lali, you fill the donkey's bucket with water," Mehrigul said, catching Lali's hands, bringing her to a stop. "I'll see what I can find for him to eat."

"No. More dancing," Lali said, looking over at Ana for support. Ana shook her head.

"Maybe later," Mehrigul said.

When they returned from the shed, Ana had put pots and pans outside, collecting precious drops of rain. Chong Ata was by the fence that separated the yard from the corn-field. Part of it had been toppled by the storm.

"If we can get the sections of fallen fence onto the roof, they will make a good rack for the food. The rain could wash away some of the dust and sand," Chong Ata said. "Do you think you can get it up there, Mehrigul?"

The sections of the fence that had collapsed were mostly undamaged, the vertical slats still held together with cross boards. And Chong Ata was right — if they laid the food piece by piece on raised platforms, the rain would help salvage it.

"That's a wonderful idea, Chong Ata." Somehow she would do it. She wouldn't tell him that their ladder had lost its top rungs. It was probably safe for the weight of a girl.

Soon Mehrigul was arranging the grid. Ana and Lali

gathered peaches from the sticky, sandy piles that had collected along the rim of the flat roof and laid them out one by one. They rescued clusters of grapes that had not yet dried to raisins, strings of red peppers, green peppers, the few remaining ears of corn. And when they'd laid out their reclaimed store, Mehrigul made Lali join her in a hunt of the area around the house for anything more they could retrieve. They found a few corncobs, but the sand-coated peach halves were only good for donkey food. Ana stayed on the roof, turning things over and over so all sides were exposed to the rain.

The rain fell for a good amount of time. Much had been lost, but much was saved, too.

By midafternoon, the sun shone. Their land would soon be dry and dusty again. Mehrigul dug her bare feet into the softened earth at the bottom of a small puddle and splashed, splattering mud all over the bottom of her pants. She didn't want Lali to see her, but it felt good. And for the first time in so long, she was free.

She rushed to the shed and hopped onto the bicycle. Pedaled down the road as fast as she could until she came to the stand of bamboo. She hid the bicycle and made her way into the grove, to her secret place. The profusion of branches and leaves from the culms had protected the ground from the worst of the blown sand. Raindrops fell from the leaves as she pushed her way through, but a little rain would do no harm to her baskets.

Halfway in, Mehrigul halted, sorry she hadn't stopped to pick up the bag of felt Pati had given her. But she'd snuck off so Lali wouldn't ask to go with her. She needed to be alone — to finally weave the vines she'd collected into the shapes she pictured in her mind.

She stopped again. Had she taken the wrong path? Mehrigul was certain this was her secret spot — her token was there, still tied to the bamboo culm; the bamboo covering she'd laid on top of her baskets was there, pushed aside. There were no baskets. She dropped to her knees, her hands groping in every direction. Could the bamboo have blown aside and the baskets been carried away by the wind? Were they nearby? The unwoven vines were there, lying in neat stacks. Just as she'd left them.

It had to be the animals. Had squirrels dragged them off, deeper into the grove, for their winter nests?

She crawled among the culms, moving in ever-widening circles around her hiding place, until she knew for certain she would not find what she was looking for. She went again to her secret spot and sank down, her arms holding her knees tight to her.

Someone had taken her baskets.

Closing her eyes helped her remember. Pati knew her secret, had come here with her. She'd gone to the trouble of getting felt for Mehrigul, expecting her to use it, giving it to her only yesterday. Pati wouldn't do such a thing, even as a tease.

Ata had been at the road when she and Pati emerged from the bamboo. They had dashed in to chase a birdcall, Pati had told him. Mehrigul had been certain he didn't believe her, but he had asked no more questions. Had taken the bicycle. Pedaled down the road.

Then she remembered colliding with Ata as he emerged from Chong Ata's workroom with the baskets he was taking to sell at Cow Horn Mountain — two bags thrown over his shoulder, one large, one small. The look on his face. He had seemed startled, but it was anger, she'd decided at the time.

Now she knew.

What she'd seen was guilt. Ata had taken her baskets.

FIFTEEN

THE HEAVY SMELL OF mutton reached Mehrigul as she crossed the yard. Ana must have made soup with the bone they'd bought at market. A special meal in celebration of the rain. A treat that at any other time she would have welcomed.

No real feeling had come back to Mehrigul since she sat stunned inside the bamboo grove, staring hopelessly at the empty spot on the ground. She had no plan. Could not wind her mind around what to do. She was filled with rage, yet her body was listless. She wanted only to sleep. To forget.

"We worried, Mehrigul. We didn't know what chores might be keeping you." Ana ladled a large spoonful of soup into a bowl and offered it to Mehrigul as soon as she'd taken her place on the floor.

Steady your hands, Mehrigul told herself. *Take the dish. Raise it to your lips. Drink the broth.*

The bowl seemed so heavy, but they were watching

her — Ana, Chong Ata, Lali. She grabbed a turnip with her fingers. Ate it greedily. An onion. A carrot. Still they watched. And cared. She was being treated as if she were the man of the house. She had done the tasks of men and was being honored.

"The soup is good, Ana," Mehrigul said, and a smile spread slowly over Ana's face. "You worked hard today. Thank you for doing this, too." And Ana had worked hard. She'd made many trips up and down the ladder, trying to restore their supply of food, scraping it, washing it bit by bit. There was a healthy glow to her cheeks that had been missing for some time.

"It will be a hard winter," Ana said, "but we'll be all right."

Ana would not have said these words if Ata were there. She was comforting them as she used to, before they were all weighed down by Ata's voiceless rage. Ata's anger had begun long ago and had grown worse when Memet left.

Tonight, when they could be alone, she would tell Ana about Ata. It was time. She would tell everything.

Mehrigul tucked Lali in early, for she had to wake at dawn and go to school. Chong Ata, too, retired early.

"Will you walk outside with me, Ana?" Mehrigul said.

Ana asked no questions. She put on a jacket and followed Mehrigul.

The blue-black silhouette of mountains stood out against the rosy tints of the afterglow that colored the sky. The ever-present haze of dust had been washed into the earth to reveal the majestic Kunlun, whose glaciers fed the streams that kept them alive. The beauty and the power of these mountains had been made known to her by Chong Ata.

She'd learned this from Ata, too, in a different way. Ata never used many words, but he was one with their land. He knew its seasons, its signs. Listened to the birds. Taught Mehrigul their names, their calls. He was no longer that person, and hadn't been for a long time. Even as a small child she sensed that things had changed for Ata, for all of them, on the day Uncle Kasim moved away for his job in Turpan. Leaving sorrow and empty, decaying spaces in their family compound. Leaving all the work of the farm to Ata. As Memet grew, he began to carry some of the burden; the spaces did not seem so empty when he was around. Now he was gone.

Mehrigul looked at Ana standing beside her, so listless, stooped under the weight of their hardships, the loneliness, and the burden that had been thrust upon her, too, when Uncle's family left, when her only son left. But Mehrigul would tell her about Ata. She should know.

"Two weeks ago, at market, an unusual thing happened, Ana. I didn't tell you about it . . . because it involved Ata in a way that was not good." Mehrigul and Ana were both looking at the sky, watching the rose color become a deeper red.

"Do you remember the silly vine basket I made? The one Memet hung on the donkey cart for decoration?" Mehrigul glanced at Ana, who kept her gaze straight ahead.

"No . . . I never noticed," Ana said with a slight shrug.

"An American lady who was at the market saw it and liked it. She bought it and offered to buy more. I've been secretly making them. She plans to come back to the market next week and buy them." The deep red of the afterglow was changing into shades of purple.

"Only . . . the baskets were stolen from me." Mehrigul forced the words out. She wanted the story told before the purple turned to total darkness. "It was . . . it was . . . Ata." Her voice caught. "He knew my hiding place. He took them to the pilgrimage market to sell. Why, Ana? Why would he do that? How could he?"

Ana clasped her hands. She shook her head slowly. "If your father took the baskets, then they were not stolen."

Mehrigul could not stifle her gasp.

"Your father would know best where to sell them," Ana said.

"No, Ana." Mehrigul swiveled to face her. "It was not best to take them to the pilgrimage market. They'll be of little value there. He knows that."

Ana backed away, her hands inching up until they were wrapped tightly around her.

"I was paid one . . . hundred . . . yuan for the basket by the American lady," Mehrigul said. Her chest heaved, but the words came clear and steady. She'd make Ana listen. "That is many times more than Chong Ata's baskets bring."

Mehrigul paced around Ana. Circled her. "Ata had spent the money we made from selling the peaches — on something else. I gave him the hundred yuan I earned so he could have our corn ground." Mehrigul stopped, until Ana's eyes met hers. "He asked me not to tell you."

Ana's mouth moved but no sound came out.

"Ata knew exactly how much my baskets might be worth."

Mother and daughter stood silent under a night sky that had begun to reveal a few stars and the slim crescent of a moon.

"Why, Ana . . . why would he take them from me?"

"Did you see him take them?" Ana said. "How do you know?"

"He ... he guessed where they were ... in the bamboo grove. He saw me come out of there with Pati. Now they're gone. And ... I saw a bag where he must have had them when he loaded the truck. I know he had them, Ana ... by the look on his face when he passed me."

"You cannot be certain, then, can you, that he took them?"

Mehrigul's hands balled in front of her. How could Ana not believe her!

"Have you thought that Pati might have taken them?" Ana said. "Didn't you say she had been in the grove with you?"

"Pati would never take them. She's helping to teach me English. She brought felt for me to weave." Mehrigul spoke faster and faster. Not believing Ana could think that of her friend, when Ata was clearly guilty.

"Perhaps Pati is no longer your friend," Ana said, a strange bitterness creeping into her voice. "Maybe it was something that girl she was with at the market set her up to do — the young girl who does not have a high opinion of us, Mehrigul."

Mehrigul closed her eyes to regain control. Ana could blame Pati, but not Ata.

"I don't think Pati, or Hajinsa, would have much use for the baskets, Ana," she said. "Nor would a man on pilgrimage. They were not useful, but that's what the lady seemed to want. She might have paid us a great many yuan for them."

Mehrigul stopped. Ana stood there with no expression on her face. As if she had no interest in hearing more.

"Listen to me, Ana." Mehrigul grabbed her mother's clutched arms. Forced them open. Put her face so close to Ana's that Ana couldn't help but hear her. "You say it's all right for Ata to take my baskets. Is it all right for him to take our money we work so hard to earn and spend it on wine? And gambling?"

Ana tried to pull away. Mehrigul tightened her grip.

"He gambles, Ana. Throws our money away on the gaming table. I've seen him. Is it all right for him to do that?"

This time Ana did not try to pull away. Or answer.

"Why is stealing our money so different from stealing my baskets? Tell me!" Mehrigul's voice pierced the stillness and hung in the air around them.

Hung in the darkness of the night that had enveloped them.

Ana leaned her face away. Stared at the ground. "Your father has a heavy heart," she said in a hushed voice. "When your brother left, he gave up all hope. The world around us is one he no longer understands."

"You're saying it's all right for us to go without food? For me to give up school? So he can wander off and drink and gamble?"

"He drinks too much. Many of your father's friends do." Ana paused. "He needs the money, Mehrigul, so he can keep his place among them, keep their friendships. It's all he has now."

"Ana," Mehrigul said, "my baskets are gone. Money you might have had to help get through the winter . . . is gone! You gave up your friends when we no longer had money. Why is this so different — that he has to steal?"

"Your father is troubled. He's not dishonest. You're wrong to accuse him." Ana pulled away, and Mehrigul let her go. Had all she could do to not push her away.

Why had Mehrigul thought Ana might change if she knew what Ata had done? She might as well have been talking to their old donkey.

She'd make more baskets. Hide them in a place no one

could possibly find. She'd meet with Mrs. Chazen. She'd buy them. Or not.

Then what? Mrs. Chazen would go back to America. Mehrigul would be sent away . . .

"Go fix yourself some tea, Ana," she said. "I'm sure you could use a good night's sleep."

SIXTEEN

Lali nestled so trustingly against her gave Mehrigul reason to begin a new day. Daylight strained into the room through dust-gray windows. How quickly the rain had given way to winds from the desert, coating the windows once again with fine grains of sand.

No one stirred. Mehrigul tucked the blanket around Lali and slid quietly from the platform. She put on pants, shirt, vest—the same dirty, gritty clothes she'd crawled out of the night before—and went about building a fire in their cookstove, grateful that there'd been a few twigs left in reserve. One of her chores today would be to collect more kindling. Nothing was left of the pile that once stood beside the house.

She walked outside to fill the kettle, then put it on to boil. She found one last piece of naan in the tin. That would be for Lali. If Mehrigul built a fire in the earth oven, maybe Ana would rally enough to bake more.

Mehrigul woke Lali with a finger to her lips. When Lali's eyes popped open, she understood and played the game of being extra quiet. She tiptoed. Hugged her favorite red and green sweater with a noiseless squeal. Her face fell when she knelt to drink tea and saw the pitiful chunk of dried naan beside it. Still, she dunked and chewed as quietly as a mouse.

Once outside, Lali pulled Mehrigul faster and faster toward the roadway. "Can I talk now?" she asked.

Mehrigul nodded.

"*Tai hao la,*" Lali said. "That's great." She grabbed Mehrigul's hands and tried to turn her round. "Do you know what I want to be?"

"*Bu zhi dao, gao su wo.* No, tell me," Mehrigul said.

"A dancer. Someone who sings and dances and is famous on television."

"How do you know about that?" Mehrigul caught Lali, tugged her close.

"My friend tells me all about it," Lali said, her cheeks flushed with excitement. "Uyghur girls can sing and dance in hotels and make lots of money. I'd live in a big city with my friend." She broke away. Twirling. Dancing with lively steps.

"You're very good, Lali," Mehrigul called. "I love to watch you. Come, give me a hug before you leave for school."

Mehrigul's arms engulfed Lali when her sister danced to her. She held Lali close until her body stilled. "You can be very popular right here, singing and dancing at weddings. You must practice and learn all the Uyghur songs." She lifted Lali's face, brushing aside the wispy bangs that peeked out from her headscarf.

"But today," Mehrigul said in Mandarin, "you will pay close attention to your studies. Get the highest marks. And be better than anyone else at speaking Mandarin. For I believe you, Lali, will make a very good teacher." She held Lali at arm's length, made sure she was listening. "That is what I want you to be."

Lali squeezed her cheeks. "Teachers are old and fussy . . . and bossy. I don't want to be one." She flipped her head from side to side.

"You have lots of time to think about it. For now, do the best you can." Mehrigul put her arm around her sister and led her to the road. The family who picked Lali up were heading toward them in their donkey cart. "We can pretend I'm your student and you can give me lessons on the important things you learn each day." Mehrigul's face lost its gentleness as she turned Lali toward her; she must make her sister understand how important it was. "That way I'll know exactly how you are doing."

Lali pulled away. "Sounds fun," she called over her shoulder as she skipped off and hopped onto the cart.

And if Mehrigul were sent away, who would guide her sister? Who would take care of her precious Lali?

Mehrigul thought only of Lali and Chong Ata as she did her chores. She hated that Ata and Ana might benefit from her work. Ata, away selling her baskets. Ana, on her sleeping platform, her body still crouched in the corner.

Mehrigul glared at Ana and gave an extra punch to the dough she was kneading. She banged pots to make as much noise as she could before slamming the door on her way outside. She had to search for dry, seasoned wood to build the fire in the earth oven.

Ana was up and dressed when Mehrigul returned. She stood looking at the bowl of dough. She seemed surprised it was there, perhaps wondering when she had made it. Which offered little promise that this would be one of Ana's good days.

"The fire's ready. Think you could bake bread for us?" Mehrigul asked, her voice coming out even nastier than she'd meant it to.

For a moment Ana looked at Mehrigul, her mouth set in a straight, hard line. Then she picked up the bowl and headed outside.

There was something in her mother's expression, in the way she walked, that made Mehrigul regret the tone she'd used. Had hearing the truth about Ata begun to unlock the self-pitying stupor Ana had chosen to live in? Maybe this jolt of reality would remind her that there were problems greater than the bitterness she harbored toward her own sad existence. With that, and her teas, could she at least begin to deal with life again? Would she ever realize how much Lali needed her?

How could Mehrigul possibly leave — be sent away — if Ana couldn't even bake naan?

Something had to happen. Soon. But right now there was only Ana to count on, and Ana had better learn to live in the real world, or Lali might end up dancing in a hotel. Or worse.

Mehrigul knew that unleashing her own anger at Ana was not helpful. For Lali's sake, she must try to support

Ana, make her more useful. Besides, she was hungry. If Ana baked, she could get a few of her own chores done.

By the time Mehrigul had sprinkled water on the earthen floors of their house and swept away the storm's dirt and sand, picked weeds from the garden and fed them to the donkey, and collected kindling from the far reaches of their farm, Ana had managed the baking. Mehrigul sat with Chong Ata, relishing the taste of the fresh naan.

The respite was short-lived. The field out by the peach trees was to be planted with winter wheat while Ata was away. Mehrigul hated the good-daughter part of herself that compelled her to do what Ata had ordered. It was to be done by his return, and today would be best. The ground had been softened by the rain.

With steps of lead, Mehrigul headed for the shed to get the hoe. Ata should be here planting wheat. Not away selling her baskets while she had only five days left to make new ones.

Resentment spread through her body like a weed, creeping into her mind as she headed for the field. What was Ata doing? Drinking? Gambling? Spending the money he made from her baskets?

Mehrigul hacked at the earth with no intent to make

neat and tidy rows, until sweat and tears clouded her eyes and she stopped. She dropped the hoe and walked away, heading for the stand of bamboo. She would make more baskets. She'd take them to the American lady. If the lady liked them . . . Mehrigul was almost afraid to think of the happiness that would bring her. It was so far removed from the life she lived right now.

She quickly retrieved the bundle of grapevines she'd stored among the bamboo culms. Squatting in the middle of her hidden retreat, she placed them before her. For a moment she closed her eyes, sat quietly until the memory of the first cone-shaped basket she'd made came to her.

"Choose five stems," she told herself. "Long enough to fold and make ten rods."

One of the sharp ends scraped her palm. "Ouch." She dropped the stem. Blood covered the cut. But she saw something that worried her more. Her hands were blotchy red and swollen from gripping the rough handle of the hoe. Would her fingers still be able to feel the hidden magic in a branch?

Even if she worked and worked, it would be years before she could make a basket that had the beauty of the one she'd seen in the museum. She wanted so badly to learn, to try. Which would be worse — working in a factory where she could make no baskets at all, or working on the farm until her hands were ruined?

With greater care, she sorted through the bundle, picking out the longest and most supple vines. Even as she set them aside, she knew they would not do. They could not be bent easily. They needed to be moistened, or she would have to cut new vines.

Mehrigul sat back on her heels, motionless, with no good plan for making even a simple basket today — if she still knew how. A shiver passed through her. She squeezed herself into a tight ball, wrapping her arms around her legs, overcome with fear that her fingers had lost their power. The vines were old and dry, and they'd taken no form in her mind. Her fingers had no urge to turn unwieldy vines into something that might be good enough to hang from a donkey cart.

She'd made so few baskets of her own. Had they really been special? Chong Ata had said he liked them, but maybe only to please her. Pati had liked them.

The thought of Pati disturbed her. She couldn't erase the picture of her walking away at the market. Her closeness with Hajinsa. Could Ana be right? Had Hajinsa schemed with Pati to steal her baskets? Hajinsa might do a thing like that, but never Pati.

Mehrigul fell back against the bamboo. She watched, unmoving, as the light that filtered through the culms began to dim. Watched as the gentle flutter of the long, narrow leaves changed, carried now by a stronger wind from the north that brought cold night air. Her token stirred with the leaves. Perhaps the favor of her wish had been used up.

No basket would be made today. And tomorrow? There were only four days left.

As she emerged from the bamboo grove she heard Lali. "Mehrigul! Mehrigul!" her sister called, her voice like the howl of a frightened animal.

Mehrigul hurried down the road. Rounding the bend, she saw Lali on the roof, turning in one direction then another, her hands cupped around her mouth, calling.

"I'm coming!" Mehrigul shouted.

Lali scrambled down the ladder and ran toward her. "Why weren't you here to meet me when I got home?" Lali wailed. "You always are. No one knew where you'd gone." She tightened her arms around Mehrigul.

The sisters stood clasped together in the middle of the road. Mehrigul felt the racing of Lali's heart. She hugged her sister closer, tighter. She'd thought it a blessing for Lali to be young, not to realize that they had a mother who could no longer cope. A father so often not there, or cross, or stumbling in his steps. But Lali did see and know all this, in her way.

"You're squeezing too tight, Mehrigul," Lali said, but she didn't try to pull away.

"Oh, Lali," Mehrigul said, holding her sister's face in her hands, planting kisses on her forehead. "Wherever I am . . . I'll always be thinking of you."

The pressure in Mehrigul's chest grew almost to bursting when she saw tears streaming from Lali's eyes. Mehrigul wiped them away with her fingers as her own eyes filled. Lali must not see her cry.

She put her arm around Lali's shoulders and guided her down the road. Lali's arm slid around Mehrigul, her sister's shirt clutched tightly in her fist.

"You do know that you're exceptionally clever, quite capable of taking care of yourself. Don't you?" Mehrigul asked. "You must remember that." She tried not to let the urgency of the message creep into her voice. Lali's innocence scared her. Mehrigul had coddled Lali when she should have been making her tough.

Lali was slowly bobbing her head as she chewed her lip. "Okay," she answered in a tearful voice.

It was a long moment before Mehrigul could find more

words, and the strength to say them. Her powerlessness to change things was not useful to Lali.

"Are you ready with my lesson for today?" she asked.

"Um-huh," Lali mumbled.

"We better begin right now, then."

"All right," Lali said, nodding agreement.

Mehrigul could feel her sister's fist loosen its grip.

"Here we go. *Jintian, wo men xue xi niao he shu*. Today we study birds and trees . . ."

SEVENTEEN

IT WAS SATURDAY. Lali was home, shadowing Mehrigul's every move, every footstep. When the chance finally came to send Lali to the garden with Ana to pick a few vegetables, Mehrigul gently pushed her sister away.

As soon as Ana and Lali left the yard, Mehrigul went to Chong Ata's workroom. "I must talk to you," she said, kneeling beside him. "It's about my baskets. I . . . I no longer have them."

Chong Ata stopped weaving.

"Ata took them with him to sell when he went on pilgrimage. He didn't ask if he could, but I'm certain he took them." The minute the words were out, the doubt, the thought that she had no real proof made her draw back. "Anyway," she said, "they're gone."

Her voice had lowered, but she knew Chong Ata had heard. It seemed as if a veil had covered his face.

"I guess I don't really know that he did. But if it was Ata who took them," Mehrigul went on, "Ana said it was his right, because he would know best what to do with them. Only ... I wanted so badly to take them to the American lady." Her outpouring of words slowed.

"I'm sorry, Chong Ata, to tell you this — to bother you. I thought I could just make more," she said. "But . . . I haven't. I'm not certain I know how anymore. My fingers ..." Mehrigul couldn't go on. She hoped Chong Ata didn't see she was crying.

He still held the basket he'd been weaving. His fingers began to work again.

"There is willow in the bundle behind me that is moist and ready to be woven," he said calmly. "Gather what you need to make a simple basket, as I do, for market."

Mehrigul's fingers, which had failed her earlier, were again swift and knowing as she followed the rhythm of Chong Ata's weaving. A wave of relief passed over her. Perhaps she had not lost her touch. "Six turnips will already fit into the base of my basket, Chong Ata. Is it time to start the sides?"

"Yes," Chong Ata said. "That will make a basket good enough for a woman to use in the kitchen."

Mehrigul smiled. Chong Ata was a wise man.

Mehrigul was still of easy mind when Lali planted herself beside her. "Help Ana in the kitchen," she told her sister. "All right, Lali? I'll be right here. We'll have time together later."

Lali stayed and chattered on. When neither her sister nor her grandfather paid any attention to her, she went inside.

Mehrigul's fingers kept their rhythm as she wove willow branches into the sides of her basket, worked the border.

When Mehrigul placed her finished basket in front of Chong Ata, he took her hands in his. Held them. Held them until they trembled beyond control. Trembled until the fragile twine that had held her together gave way to a desperation she could no longer keep inside.

Chong Ata's grip tightened and held fast while Mehrigul fought to catch her breath through the sobs that shook her body.

When her gulps for air turned into a deep sigh, Chong Ata loosened his hold. His fingers caressed her hands.

"Your fingers have not lost their magic. What is still bothering you, Granddaughter?"

Knowing that he cared, that he understood, she wrapped her arms around him in a hug of relief.

"Oh, Chong Ata," she said. "The American lady comes in four days. I have only three days left to make baskets."

She sat back on her heels. "Ata will be here tomorrow and then I'll have to do it in secret. He's forbidden me to make more baskets. He says it's useless, that the lady won't come back anyway.

"But I still want to!" she cried. "More than anything I've ever cared about."

Chong Ata sat quietly, studying Mehrigul. His head shook slowly. "Cut new vines," he said. "They will be supple. You can begin to work right away. Remember, they'll shrink when they dry. You must account for that."

He put the knife that was at his side into Mehrigul's hand. "Go now," he said. "I'll speak to your mother and keep your sister busy."

With an armful of fresh-cut grapevines, Mehrigul settled right where she was, in front of the patch. As she began to trim the vines, cutting off leaves, she decided to strip them, to peel away the shreddy bark. She liked the smoother feeling. She'd start again with a cornucopia, but the one she made today would be more refined, less rustic than the one Mrs. Chazen had bought. She was still careful to leave all the tendrils that grew from the leaf scars. The wispy spirals would add a special touch.

When the rods and weavers, trimmed and cut to size, were in place before her, she sat back. She closed her eyes but did not pray. She listened for the sounds of silence, like the rustle of autumn leaves being stirred by the breeze. She breathed in the sweet smell of a rotting peach that had somehow escaped their harvest. This was the peace she needed to begin her work.

Mehrigul opened her eyes. There, before her, was the peach orchard with its almost bare branches. To the far side of the orchard was the untilled field. And in the field was the hoe she'd cast aside.

"No." She shook her head back and forth. "I'll make three baskets. Then I'll prepare the field. This is my work, Ata!"

Within a short time Mehrigul was passing weavers through the rods. Mindful of Chong Ata's caution, she made a looser weave, trying to envision what it might become when the moisture left the vines and the basket became smaller. She was comforted by the realization that the cornucopia she'd made before had looked all right, when she wasn't even thinking it might shrink.

Her hands didn't flow with the same grace she'd felt while working with Chong Ata. She thought that must be because of the more rugged vine. Willow was easier to move about.

She ran out of weavers. She stopped, prepared more, growing anxious that it was taking longer than she'd hoped.

Again, she squeezed her eyes shut. She must stop her heart from racing. Calm her breathing.

"All right," she whispered to herself. "Two baskets. I'll try to make two."

Mehrigul picked up a weaver. There was a slight tremor in her hands, but her stomach rumbled and she thought the trembling could be caused by hunger. She knew how to go without food. That was not as hard as forgetting about the thrown-down hoe. About Ata. About the baskets she no longer had to show to Mrs. Chazen.

Again Mehrigul forced herself to block out everything but the sounds around her — the faint buzz of a bee, the scampering of a squirrel. Loudest was the chatter of birds. Feeding. It was their feeding time — and she'd not made even one basket.

Nothing mattered now but finishing. She had at least five centimeters to add before beginning the border. As quickly as she could, she worked the weavers. In. Out. In. Out. In. Out. Round and round and round. She widened the rods as she came closer and closer to the top. Her hand cramped. She rubbed her fingers. Pushed on.

The border. And finally, a small handle to hang it from. Her donkey-cart basket had that. Mrs. Chazen would want a handle. She bent a thin rod in half, attached it to the border. Plaiting the two parts, she created a short arch and fastened it to the other end.

Mehrigul placed the finished work in front of her.

Her basket looked like a bunch of ugly sticks.

She folded her hands in front of her. Took another look. Much of the weaving was even. It held a good cone shape. Mehrigul grabbed the basket. She used the knife to fix spaces that were too wide or too narrow. She hid the loose ends that had escaped when she'd begun to use a new weaver.

Again she placed the basket on the ground and stared at it. Then at her hands. She was confused. They'd done what she told them to. They'd made a basket. Only . . . not a basket worthy of a hundred yuan. She knew that.

There was no grace, no beauty in what she'd made.

"Why?" She asked herself the question but had no answer.

She tried to envision the cornucopia she'd made for Memet. As she saw it more clearly in her mind's eye, her face released into a soft smile. Now she knew. She had woven happiness into her basket for Memet.

She looked at the cornucopia in front of her. Anger had been woven into this basket.

Mehrigul raised herself from the ground and with the heel of her shoe crushed the basket into the earth.

EIGHTEEN

WILL THERE BE SQUASH to take to market on Wednesday, Ana?" Mehrigul said as the family sat at breakfast.

Ana finished sipping her tea, laid down the bowl. "The few that are left we'll need for ourselves."

"What will we take, then? Chong Ata has baskets ready, but would Ata go with only baskets?" Mehrigul tried to hide her alarm. They had to go to market. She hadn't thought about what might happen after the harvest. Ata and Memet had always worried about that before. She'd been at school.

"It's time to sell cornstalks and husks," Ana said. "Only" — she looked away — "your father . . . he'll be upset. So much was scattered by the wind."

"Why didn't you say so? We could have picked them up. Had it done before he returns today. He could be here any minute." Mehrigul jumped to her feet. "Eat up, Lali," she said. "We have a job to do."

"Who'd want to buy cornhusks?" Lali asked as she stuffed a large piece of naan into her mouth.

"People who want food for their donkeys, or goats, or sheep." Mehrigul thrust her hand out to Lali. Pulled her up. "That's why I went to the trouble of peeling the husks from every single cob of corn we grew . . . and put them in a neat pile."

Mehrigul dragged Lali over to get their jackets. "So," she said, "you and I are going out to pick up the stalks and husks that blew away." She looked over her shoulder. "How about you, Ana? Will you help? Or sit all day with your tea?" Mehrigul hadn't planned for her words to be cold-hearted. But if Ana was worried about how Ata would react, why hadn't she been out picking up husks? She wasn't an invalid.

Or maybe she was, Mehrigul thought.

Ana's hands stayed clasped tight, in front of her.

When Mehrigul stooped to grab the naan that was still at her place, she saw Chong Ata's head bowed low. For his sake, she regretted what she'd said. But she wouldn't take it back.

She headed for the door.

* * *

"We'll count every time we pick up a stalk," Lali announced. "That will be your lesson for today, Mehrigul." Many of the stalks had been blown only a short distance from the neat, round stack. "*Yi, er,*" she counted in Mandarin, picking up those nearest and throwing them onto the pile.

Mehrigul retrieved the stalks. "As they grow — bottom to top round the pile," she said, replacing them. "That is the way it's done."

Lali shrugged.

"*San, si, wu, liu, qi, ba, jiu,*" Mehrigul said, placing more against the pile.

Lali scurried away. Picked up more. "*Shi, shiyi, shier,*" she sang out.

The game went on. That is what it was. For a while there was almost joy in running around with her sister, seeing who could pick up the most stalks and count the fastest.

"*Sanbai,* three hundred!" Lali's voice was triumphant. She'd run a distance with her one stalk to say the big number.

"There're more out there. Let's each get two more armloads. Then we'll start picking up husks."

"No," Lali groaned, sinking to the ground. "I'm tired.

You said I should be a teacher. What good is it to know how to do this?"

Mehrigul hunched down next to Lali. She took the naan from her pocket. Broke off half and gave it to her. "We do this because it brings us money, and money is needed to buy your books and other things."

Lali with a crumpled face was so sweet, and so sad. "Why are you looking at me like that, Mehrigul?"

"Because, when you pout, you're adorable." Mehrigul put her arms around her sister, hugged her close.

"No," Lali said, trying to break away. "I mean it. I don't want to work anymore."

"It has to be done, and I don't want to do it alone. That's fair, isn't it?"

Lali shook her head. "I guess so."

"Enough rest, then," Mehrigul said. "Two more armfuls of stalks. Then we'll use sacks to collect the husks — the big one for me, the small one for you — and start way back in the peach orchard. Husks fly like birds with the wind behind them."

And Lali became a bird, swooping and flapping across the stubble of the cornfield, gliding under the branches of the peach trees.

When they returned, dragging their bags across the field, Ana was picking up husks near the house. Lali ran ahead, opening her bag to show Ana all she'd collected. From the movement of Lali's arms and body, Mehrigul knew she was telling Ana how husks could fly.

Ana was still holding Lali close when Mehrigul reached them. She tried to bring back a memory of a time when Ana had held her. None came. Mehrigul had been a disappointment. Ata had hoped for another boy. She knew from Memet that Ata blamed Ana for having a girl. That, and she was certain she'd never been as cute and lovable as Lali. Even Ata seemed to like Lali and let her get away with things.

Mehrigul worked at the far ends of the corn stubble. Ana and Lali stayed closer to the pile, picking husks at a slower pace, both looking out toward the road whenever they straightened up. Soon Mehrigul did it, too — watched for Ata to come down the road. Listened for the rumble of the truck.

The longer they waited for Ata's return, the more Ana wandered about, forgetting to pick up husks. Slipping further and further into that place she went, that lifeless place where she could escape the realities of her world.

"Take Ana into the house, Lali," Mehrigul said at last. "Help her prepare food. Ata will want to eat when he comes home."

After collecting another full bag, Mehrigul took the emptied sacks to the shed. She'd done enough, and knew no reason why she must wait around for Ata's return when she could be making a basket. She went to Chong Ata for a moment. Watched him weave. She didn't speak to him about her failure. Nor did she allow herself to think she might fail again.

"Chong Ata, may I borrow your knife?" It was lying on the ground in front of him. She knew he wouldn't need it for a while. "I need to cut more vines," she said.

He nodded. "Use it well, Granddaughter. It is now *our* knife." He reached for it and placed it in Mehrigul's hands.

Mehrigul knew that her grandfather believed she could make a good basket — expected her to.

She was careful to choose branches that were straight and slender, that bent easily around her fist. She was patient with herself as she stripped the vines. With an ample supply, she picked up the bundle and walked to her hidden spot in the bamboo grove.

Alone and sheltered, Mehrigul crossed her hands over

her heart and bowed her head. She had never been inside a mosque to pray, or heard other women, even her mother, pray aloud. Yet she always felt at peace when she was beside Chong Ata while he prayed. She sought that peace, that stillness for her mind and body, though she knew no special words to help her. As her eyes opened, she saw her token, the piece of white cloth she had tied to the bamboo culm. That seemed so long ago, she'd almost forgotten. The white cotton had become gray with settled dust and sand. She touched it now. Wanting so much to believe there was enough power left to bring the knowledge of beauty to her fingers once again.

Her mind was soon planning the basket she would make. Something worth one hundred yuan. But the thought of money, the idea that her work would warrant that large amount, overwhelmed her. There was so much she didn't know. What kind of baskets did other people make? She had no books, no place to go to learn. How had she thought she could make more baskets Mrs. Chazen would like?

"Stop!" she shouted. Angry. Angry at herself. "You made three baskets. You can do it again." It was easier to believe, saying it out loud. "You learned at Chong Ata's side. Your fingers know how to work."

She'd wasted precious time. Yet she forced herself to work slowly. Deliberately. She chose the best vines to use for rods and began.

It was late but she worked on. The core secure, she picked a long, thin vine and started weaving the bottom of the cone.

Then she heard it. The sound they'd listened for all day. And knew she had to be there to meet Ata the minute he got out of the truck. The look in his eyes would tell her if he'd taken her baskets. She had to know.

Mehrigul sprinted across the fields, careful to stay out of sight of the road. She could outrun the sputtering, broken-down truck. The louder the noise, the faster she ran. What would she see when Ata stepped down from the truck?

She broke into a smile. What if Ata hadn't been able to sell her baskets and had brought the useless things home?

The door on the passenger side of the truck opened before the dust it had stirred up settled. Ata lurched out, balanced himself, squared his shoulders, and walked around to the driver's side.

Mehrigul couldn't hear what was said from where she

stood, leaning against the house. The exchange was brief. There was no handshake. Ata did not address Osman's sons, who sat with their legs hanging over the end of the truck bed. When Ata turned, the taller one jumped down and took his place beside his father. The other son stayed in back.

Ata carried nothing with him as he walked slowly, unsteadily, toward the house. Nothing. Not even the emptied sacks they needed for their work on the farm.

Lali ran from the house to greet him.

Mehrigul flinched when she saw Lali cover her nose and move away as Ata reached his arms toward her. There was little doubt that he had spent money on wine.

With dogged and unfaltering steps, Mehrigul narrowed her eyes and closed in on him. She didn't want Lali there, but that wasn't enough to stop her.

Ata saw her — and looked away. But Mehrigul had seen all she needed to see.

"How much did you sell my baskets for?"

Ata's shoulders jerked up and down. Finally, he faced her. Spit on the ground. "Those worthless things." He swiped his hand across his face. "Huh. They sold for less than Chong Ata's baskets. Nobody wanted them."

"Why didn't you bring them back? The American lady might have paid a good price for them." Mehrigul struggled to keep calm as she unleashed the words.

She could hear her sister's whimpers as Lali huddled against her. Mehrigul put her arm around Lali's shoulders but kept her eyes on Ata. Bands of steel seemed to tighten around her head as she fought to control herself.

"Crybabies," Ata muttered.

He started to move around them. Pulling Lali with her, Mehrigul blocked the way.

Ata glared at Mehrigul with empty black eyes. "Stop your dreaming and do some real work," he said. "I told you. Your American lady won't come back."

NINETEEN

WEAR YOUR BEST CLOTHES today, Lali. That will help make you happy." Mehrigul held out Lali's red leggings. "Red is a good color for you."

Lali had been no more than an inch away from Mehrigul since Ata's return the day before. It was Monday. She had to go to school. "Don't dawdle. Plaid skirt, red sweater. Then I'll braid your hair," Mehrigul said.

She was fixing breakfast when the door flung open. Ata stormed in, brandishing a hoe, and lashed out at Mehrigul. "The field—it's not planted. What have you been doing, girl? Making more useless baskets?"

Mehrigul straightened, ready to lash back. Narrowed her eyes as she held in her breath, searching for the right answer—until the room began to spin. She felt dizzy. As if in a daze. "I've been trying to," she said, her voice barely audible.

Ata pounded the hoe on the earthen floor. "We live on a farm. Remember?" he yelled.

Slowly, Chong Ata rose from the rug where he was sitting, having his morning tea. "I will go to the field," he said. "There are things I can do to help."

Mehrigul stifled the cry that tore at her throat. She'd made this happen. It was her fault, and she couldn't do anything to change that now.

"Not you, Chong Ata," Ata said. "These other lazy things will work until it's done. Get moving, Mehrigul. And you, Aynisa. You can work today."

Ana stood as cowed as Mehrigul. Didn't Ata know that having her in the field was as pointless as sowing seeds in the desert? Even so, Mehrigul was relieved Ana would be there. She didn't want to be alone with Ata.

Ata headed toward Lali, who had crouched against the wall, trying to hide. He put his hand on her shoulder. "Get out of those fancy clothes. You can help, too. It's time you learned. You don't need school today."

"Lali will not work in the field. She'll go to school." Suddenly, Mehrigul was standing in front of Lali, shielding her. Chong Ata had tried to protect her. She would protect Lali.

Ata raised the hoe in warning as Lali screamed and flung her arms around Mehrigul's back. Mehrigul held her stand, as deep-rooted in the earthen floor beneath her feet as a tamarisk in the desert. *Bend,* she told herself, *but do not break.* She was young; she had that strength. And Chong Ata's love.

Ata's face twisted. Finally, he stood aside, still gripping the hoe, as Mehrigul led Lali outside.

When Mehrigul returned to the house, Ata and Ana had left for the field. Chong Ata still knelt on the rug, his bowl of tea and the naan in front of him untouched. Mehrigul poured warm tea into bowls and knelt beside Chong Ata, putting aside his bowl that had grown cold.

"We must eat, Chong Ata. We need our strength."

Chong Ata's eyes were fixed on the intricate pattern in the rug, though Mehrigul doubted he was seeing it.

"It's all right. Really," Mehrigul said. "I should have done what Ata asked. I knew he'd be angry — and I let it happen." She found her own eyes directed toward the rug. "I didn't mean to get everyone else involved."

"Have you prepared more baskets to take to the American lady?"

Mehrigul didn't want to tell Chong Ata the truth. But she wouldn't lie. "No. I . . . seem to be having trouble making one. I have one started, though," she added quickly. "I'd hoped to have many." She sat back on her haunches.

"I'm not certain it matters. Maybe Ata's right. He's sure the American lady will not come back."

For a moment, Chong Ata and Mehrigul sat in silence. Then Chong Ata picked up his tea. "We should drink our tea while it is warm," he said. He drank from his bowl, then dipped naan into his tea and ate it.

Mehrigul knew to be patient. Chong Ata would have a purpose for his silence. She dipped naan into her tea, forcing down the food.

Chong Ata placed his bowl on the eating cloth. He studied her, his eyes searching her face. She knew what he was looking for, that he wouldn't speak until he thought her mind was free. How could she not be anxious about having a basket ready for Mrs. Chazen with just two days left? How could she not be afraid of Ata striking her with his hoe? She no longer knew the man she called her ata.

It was more. While her eyes burned with resentment of Ata, her mind could only find disappointment in her own failure to achieve what she so deeply desired. And Chong Ata knew.

Mehrigul lowered her head. She didn't want him to see any more. She could not find within herself the inner peace he sought. "I will go, Chong Ata, and do what I have to do.

I'll work in the field. I cannot be at one with myself until the task I left undone is completed."

She slung the hoe that had been left by the door over her shoulder and headed for the field.

Ata and Ana had started at the far end. Mehrigul was left with the uneven rows she'd carelessly turned a few days ago. They were of no use now. She stomped over them, flattening the ground, and began again. Digging deeper this time to find moistened earth that would help to nurture the seeds. Careful to furrow neat, even rows. She stopped at the end of each row to take seeds from Ana and do the planting, too. Ana was already struggling to keep up with Ata. As angry as Mehrigul was at everyone, she saw no use in letting Ana slow them down.

High noon passed and still the job was unfinished. Both Mehrigul's half and Ata's, for he'd slipped away early on. Mehrigul wondered why he'd bothered to come to the field at all. It was clearly her job to plant the field whether he was here or not. And she would, even though the pain from the blisters on her hands grew more intense with each row. Splinters from the rough wooden handle gouged her flesh, yet she worked on.

When Ana could no longer stand, she sat at the edge

of the field, holding the seed bag. Mehrigul took it from her after each new row had been prepared.

"It's about time for Lali to come home," Mehrigul said finally. "Go, Ana. Stay with her. Tell her she must not come to me. That I'll be home shortly." Mehrigul's words lacked compassion, for she felt none. Ana had to take care of Lali.

Ana nodded and left.

Though it was late when Mehrigul finished, she headed for the bamboo grove, gently stretching her hands in front of her, trying to ease the pain that shot through them. The unfinished basket lay there. If Ata had come again to steal her work, he had found it unworthy of being taken.

She squatted in front of the basket, deciding what length she'd make it, the width at the top. She regretted not having Chong Ata's knife. She wouldn't be able to finish the border. It would have been nice, too, to have water to soak the weavers, to make them softer, easier to work. She'd do without both.

Mehrigul willed herself to feel no pain as she picked up a weaver. This one would be hard to work. The rods near the bottom were so close together. The work so fine. She held her breath and pushed the vine through. It would be easier as she got nearer the top. It had to be.

Her fingers, always quick and sure, were almost impossible to move. Her hands were bleeding. There'd be blood on the basket.

It would be stained with her blood.

Mehrigul fell onto her side. She licked her fingers. Licked away the blood, but it kept coming back. She folded her hands inside her shirt and lay there.

Cold.

Defeated.

Mehrigul held her hands under the spigot. The cool water soothed them, and she might have stayed there, wasting water and not caring, if Lali had not spotted her and run outside, flung her arms around Mehrigul.

"My hands are wet; I can't hug you back right now," Mehrigul said. "But I love you. You know that, don't you?"

"Um-hum, but I'm glad you're back. No one inside is talking. Not to me. Not to anyone." Lali tightened her embrace. "Ata came home," she whispered. "He ate and went to bed. He smelled awful again."

Mehrigul bent down and nuzzled her head against Lali. "It's good he went to sleep," she whispered into Lali's ear.

She wanted to hold this moment forever, wrapped close

together with her sister, protecting her. How long would she be here to do that? Mehrigul had no answer. But she'd do everything within her power to keep Lali in school.

"Have you done your homework?" she asked as they walked through the yard.

"Yes."

"Good. Did you help Ana with supper?"

"Yes, and everyone has eaten but us. Ana said I could wait for you."

For once, Mehrigul welcomed the dim light inside the house. Low moans and raspy snores came from Ata. Chong Ata knelt on a platform, perhaps asleep, she couldn't tell. Ana busied herself by the food shelf, washing bowls. She didn't acknowledge them.

Lali scooted to a place on the rug and motioned for Mehrigul to come beside her.

"Please fill a bowl for me," Mehrigul said softly, which Lali did with no fuss, spooning *polo* into it and putting it in her sister's lap. Mehrigul leaned over the bowl and for a moment ate greedily, scooping up the rice until the salt stung the raw tips of her fingers and she could not go on.

"You eat the rest of mine," she whispered to her sister. "It'll be good for you."

This time when Mehrigul licked her fingers, it made

them feel worse. She forced herself to stay until Lali finished. "You get ready for bed," she said. "I need to go outside."

"I do too. I'm coming with you."

After they'd peed into the hole at the edge of the yard, Mehrigul shooed Lali toward the door. "You go in. My hands are sore," she said. "I must let some water run over them. I'll be right here, Lali, if you need me."

There was little comfort this time from the chill of the water.

When Mehrigul went back inside, Lali was already on their platform, her head nestled on her pillow. Ana, too, had lain down. It was Chong Ata who sat, awake, on the side of a platform.

"Show me your hands," he said, and Mehrigul knew Lali had said enough for Chong Ata to guess the truth. She held out her hands.

"There are herbs that will help. I'll grind them and make a paste."

Chong Ata got up and removed three small wooden boxes from their place above the food shelf, scooped a portion from each into a bowl, and ground the herbs with a pestle. He added water to make a smooth paste and spread it over Mehrigul's fingers and palms. He went to Ana's sewing box and took out soft white cotton, which he cut into strips and wrapped loosely around Mehrigul's hands. "This will begin the healing," he said.

He touched her forehead with his fingers, until she lifted her face. "We will see what tomorrow brings."

"Thank you, Chong Ata," she said, trying to keep the pain and the hope that was lost from showing in her voice.

When Mehrigul was certain Chong Ata was sleeping, she fixed some of Ana's tea for herself and drank it. She knew what tomorrow would bring. Her only wish now was to sleep.

TWENTY

MEHRIGUL WOKE AT DAWN, groggy from deep sleep. She brought her hands up to rub her eyes and felt the bandages. There was pain as she laid her fingers and palms against her cheeks, but no smell of blood. The throbbing had quieted.

Mehrigul inched out of bed, surprised to see she was fully clothed, with no memory of how she got to bed the night before.

She stood by the window. Unraveled the bandages. Her left hand appeared somewhat normal, but not her right hand. The loose skin that hung from the broken blisters did little to protect the tender flesh underneath. She opened and closed her fingers, testing to see what her stiff, swollen hands could do.

It didn't matter anymore. She'd resigned herself to doing whatever Ata asked, at least with her left hand, in her own time.

The other members of the household began to stir.

Mehrigul tucked the bandages into her sleeve, slid into her shoes, and went outside to gather kindling. By the time she returned, Ana was up and had Lali dressing for school.

"Would you start the fire this morning, Ana?"

Ana didn't ask why. She took the sling that held the sticks from Mehrigul's arm. Mehrigul busied herself getting water, preparing rose-hip tea, making things as normal as possible for Lali, who moved in silence, her lips quivering when Ata came to take his place at breakfast.

Only Chong Ata sat calmly, eating with steady determination. He didn't seem interested in knowing how she was, though her eyes sought his.

Mehrigul would eat, too. She wanted tea. She gripped the bowl with her left hand but had to press it against her right palm to lift it. She swallowed her gasp as pain shot through her. She couldn't do it.

If anyone saw, they made no comment.

The naan lay in broken chunks on the eating cloth. She soaked a piece in her tea, leaving it longer than usual before bringing it to her mouth. That was the way she'd have tea this morning.

Ata sat back, still chewing on naan. "Hurry up, Mehrigul," he said. "There's a lot to do to get ready for market. Bind the cornstalks first. Make plenty of bundles. We may want to make two trips tomorrow. And don't make them too generous; they'll sell for the same."

"Mehrigul will not be able to help you today," Chong Ata said. "She needs time to perform another task, and to heal her hands." There was a power in Chong Ata's voice that didn't seem to come from his frail body.

Ata stood to his full height, towering over them. An ugly smirk crossed his face. "Listen," he said, cocking his ear toward Chong Ata. "There's thunder in the air. The old man storms, and look." He pointed to the window. "No rain." He laughed. "There's nothing there."

Ata's eyes flashed as he lunged at Mehrigul. Grabbed her hands. "A few blisters? Good. When they turn to calluses you'll be worth your salt." He pushed her hands away. "Now get busy. You're a peasant. Do your job."

"No, my son. You have overstepped," Chong Ata said. "Remember the words of our sacred text: 'Our God will take you to task for what your heart has amassed.' It is time for you to listen to God's message of kindness and compassion toward others."

His words slowed time.

No one moved—until Ata locked his arms across his chest and rushed from the house.

Lali's whimpers filled the silence.

"Hold her, Ana," Mehrigul ordered. "Can't you see that Lali needs us? Needs you." She glared at Ana — and at her own wounded hands. "You must help," she pleaded. "Hold Lali while I get a cloth to wipe her face."

Lali had to go to school. She couldn't stay home today, no matter how she felt. Whatever was to happen with Ata wouldn't be good.

Ana had her arms around Lali by the time Mehrigul returned to hold a damp cloth against her forehead. Lali's body relaxed as Mehrigul wiped away her tears.

"It's time to go to the road. Are you ready?" Mehrigul said.

"I want to stay here."

"Not today. There may be something very important to learn, and how can you teach me, if you don't know?"

Lali shook her head, but Mehrigul knew she'd go.

"Ana and I will both walk with you to the road. All right?" She studied both of them as she said this. Ana nodded, even if Lali did not. For whatever good Ana might do, Mehrigul wanted her there in case they came upon Ata when they went outside.

Chong Ata sat drinking tea. Mehrigul was certain his stand had taken a toll on him, but he seemed at peace. She went to him now. Knelt beside him. "Thank you, Chong Ata," she said, biting her lips to hold back tears. She was no better than Lali. All she wanted to do was cry and sit there with her grandfather.

Chong Ata's hand gripped Mehrigul's arm. His strong fingers tightened and held her. Her pent-up hate and fear — and love — began to flow from her in quiet weeping.

"Come to my workroom when you return," he said as he loosened his hold.

Surely Chong Ata understood that she could do no weaving today. Mehrigul had accepted that when she left her unfinished, bloodied basket in the grove. If Mrs. Chazen did come looking for her tomorrow, she'd dart among the carts and hide. Still, Chong Ata's defiance was giving her hands a chance to heal, and she was grateful.

Chong Ata was busy in the back of his room when she entered. Then he came to squat beside her with strips of bamboo in his hands. He handed her one strip. "Feel this, Mehrigul. It's supple and flexible. You may be able to work with it today."

"Oh, Chong Ata." The piece she held in her left hand was creamy yellow with a shiny surface. So smooth, so perfect. A long, narrow weaver half the width of her little finger, the exact same width from top to bottom. "Where did you get this?"

"When I could no longer go into the desert to collect tamarisk, I began to make willow baskets, as I still do today. But none have been as prized or as satisfying to me as those I used to make from tamarisk."

Chong Ata shrugged as if casting off a memory and looked at the bamboo Mehrigul held in her hand. "My father was a master craftsman," he said. "He taught me how to prepare and make baskets from all the bounty of our land." Chong Ata paused and shrugged again. "I tried to make baskets from bamboo, since we had the grove nearby. I liked the process of preparing the bamboo; it kept me busy on long winter days when you and Memet were in school. I never made a basket worthy of keeping, none as masterful as his. And a woman working in a kitchen seems to prefer a simple willow basket."

"I don't understand how this strip, something so perfect and flexible, can come from a bamboo culm," Mehrigul said. "We cut grapevines and willow branches and use them just as they are."

"Once the culms are dried, they must be leached by heating them over a fire many times. I would do that after your ana was through baking naan. Next I split the culm in half, then in half again and again until I get the width of the weaver I want to use. Then I strip it by shaving off the inner and outer surfaces until each piece is smooth and of even thickness."

There was contentment on Chong Ata's face as he talked about preparing the bamboo. Mehrigul knew how it felt to trim a vine to make a weaver. Perhaps she herself was beginning to understand the joy and wonder of making things with her hands. Chong Ata had found his peace in his basket making. Would she ever find that peace?

Mehrigul held up the strip her grandfather had given her. "This is beautiful in itself, Chong Ata," she said.

"It will not be as difficult to manage as grapevine or willow. Your hands may be able to weave a simple basket from this. The spirit and soul of the maker will give it beauty. Let me take your hands, Mehrigul."

She laid the bamboo on her lap and held out her hands. No matter how dim his vision, Chong Ata would see the uselessness of her right hand — of both, really.

"It will be sore, but you must try to work."

The bowl of special salve from the night before sat beside a stack of baskets. He applied it to her hands.

"I have the cotton with me," Mehrigul said.

Chong Ata wrapped it carefully around her fingers and her palms, as if it were gloves.

"I've fixed a bag of bamboo strips for you. They've been soaking, but you'll need to have water nearby to keep them soft. Where will you feel safe to work? Of course, you may stay here with me if that's best."

It wouldn't matter. She couldn't work anywhere. Didn't Chong Ata know that? But she couldn't disappoint him. She must at least try.

"I . . . I don't know," she said, her eyes moistening with tears she had no will to hold back. "There's no place. I couldn't work anywhere near Ata."

"I understand," Chong Ata said. He rose, collected the bag he had ready for Mehrigul, and brought it to her. "Pati's family will welcome you. The miller and his wife have long been our friends. You may find peace at the stream beside the mill."

Chong Ata knelt, again, beside Mehrigul. "Are you able to ride there?"

"Yes," she said. And for a moment it almost seemed possible — that she might have a basket ready by tomorrow. "Thank you for believing I can do it."

* * *

Minutes later, in the cleaner of her two pairs of pants and a warm shirt, the bag of bamboo swinging from the handlebars, Mehrigul rode away.

The words of the old proverb tormented her. The one Ata would not let her forget. *Do not follow your heart's feelings and desires. They will cleave you like an apple and throw you away in the desert.*

Mehrigul's heart kept telling her that she would, somehow, keep making baskets. Maybe not today, but she could never give up. If Mrs. Chazen hadn't come, she might never have known she could do it. That she wanted to so very much.

No matter where the cadre sent her, she'd find something to weave. She'd keep her fingers nimble and busy with whatever piece of twine or cloth she could find. Or bark from a tree. Or grasses from beside a stream. If they sent her to a city that had a museum, maybe there would be baskets on display for her to see.

She pedaled faster toward the millstream, hoping the proverb held no truth for her.

TWENTY-ONE

MEHRIGUL DRANK TEA WITH Pati's mother and grand-mother in the warm welcome of their home. They didn't ask about her bandaged hands but found a small bowl she could manage. Pati had told them about the baskets she'd made, and it pleased Mehrigul to learn how much her friend had admired them. Pati wasn't a good secret keeper, for she had made a promise to tell no one about them, but she was a loyal friend.

Pati's mother and grandmother were honored, they said, to have Mehrigul work by the millstream. They carried a felt rug to place over the rough stones that lined the bank, so that she would be comfortable.

It took a moment for Mehrigul to dismiss her guilt for even considering the possibility that Pati had stolen her baskets. The soothing sounds of water spilling from the mill brought calm. Trees grew along the banks of the stream, and she caught an autumn leaf gliding through the air in a lazy pattern. She let the contentment she had always felt here seep through her.

She'd think of nothing but weaving a plain basket, as she had so often done at Chong Ata's side. The beauty of the bamboo would make it special for Mrs. Chazen.

Removing strips from the bag, arranging them in the form of a cross, turning them so the shiny side would be on the outside — these things were done easily with her left hand. Lightly touching her thumb to the fingers of her right hand did not bring pain, but the swelling and stiffness were still there. She'd work slowly.

Mehrigul removed her shoes. Even the beautiful bamboo would be held with her bare feet.

She pulled another strip from the bag, this one to be the weaver. It was still pliant. It was time to begin.

The bandage did nothing to protect her raw sores. The force needed to work the weaver under the spokes sent unbearable pain through her whole hand. "No!" she cried. She'd never be able to do the tight weaving necessary to build the core.

Mehrigul sat back, nursing her hand, waiting for the throbbing to stop. She had to keep going. She must. The sides would be easier.

Steeling herself, she began to chant. "Under . . . over . . . under . . . over . . ." Even through her tears she could see blood seeping through the cloth. She grabbed the weaver with her left hand, putting it over, trying to force it under . . .

Mehrigul closed her eyes until the image of Chong Ata, squatting in the yard, was clear in her mind. Chong Ata with ten fingers flying in and out, not thinking which would lift, which would push. His two hands, together, building the core. Isn't that what she'd always done, without even thinking?

Not today. This was not a day for weaving. That was a fact she must accept. Pangs shot through her left hand now. She'd not heeded the truth of the proverb. Her heart *had* been foolish and unwise. Her hopes and dreams unreal.

Ata had known the truth about her all along.

So had Hajinsa. "Yes, Hajinsa!" Mehrigul cried out to the trees. "I am nothing but a simple peasant with my scarf tied under my chin. The kind they send away to work in factories."

Mehrigul untangled what little work had been done, straightening the long strips, laying them together across her lap. She gathered the rest of the bamboo from the bag and laid that, too, on her lap. Just looked at it. Maybe someday she'd learn to prepare bamboo, make her own bamboo baskets.

She leaned back on her elbows. She was dreaming again. That chance had passed. The cadre and his wife would be the ones to decide her future.

She was a failure. She had failed to achieve the most modest of her dreams — to have just one simple basket to show Mrs. Chazen.

Mehrigul knew the punishment for dreaming. She'd be sliced like an apple, thrown to the desert. Or far away to the south. It didn't matter which. Either seemed good punishment for a foolish dreamer.

She sat staring at the stream. Watching as it spilled from the ancient stone walls of the mill and cascaded over its bed of stones. Rippling, forming patterns as it flowed by. Strange, the comfort it gave her.

Reluctant to leave but thinking she must not sit idly, Mehrigul gathered the ends of the bamboo weavers and brought them up together, cradling them in her arms. They almost became a basket, a collection of long, straight bamboo spokes forming a circle of graceful beauty that seemed to flow toward the sky.

Mehrigul held them. She couldn't let them go. She

loved the simplicity, the perfection of the bamboo and the peace it brought her. It was as if the bamboo was telling her it didn't want to be woven, it wanted to be free. As free as the culms in the grove.

How could she keep the bamboo like this without holding it in her arms? Nothing she'd ever seen had that teaching. Yet there had to be a way.

She studied the bottom of the basket—that was what she called it, for it was a basket. But it needed some kind of base or it wouldn't stand upright. Maybe if she arranged the bamboo into many piles and crisscrossed the piles one on top of the other until they looked like a wheel . . . a wheel with many spokes and a kind of woven-together center . . . then she'd bring the spokes together in four clusters . . . and wrap the bottom of each cluster with a bit of bamboo to make a sturdy base . . .

She saw her basket in her mind, and it made her smile.

As hesitant as she was to let go of the bamboo, she laid it out flat on the rug. First she made sure, as Chong Ata had instructed, that every strip was turned so the shiny surface would be seen on the outside. Then she built her wheel, using a few strips at a time.

Mehrigul looked at her hands. The hard part would

be pulling the bamboo around the center into four clusters and binding each cluster with bamboo. She took four strips and dipped them into the millstream. Held them in the water until they were soft and pliable, and then she began.

There was pain. There was much pain, but her plan seemed to work. She bound each cluster about four centimeters away from the center, wrapping it around and around with the bamboo strip until it became a little foot. Four small feet around the crisscrossed center would be the base of her basket.

Now she needed something to take the place of her arms holding the bamboo upright. She decided to make a loose braid with three strips of the bamboo — if her fingers would let her. She chose new strips and again dipped them into the stream to make them as supple as possible.

She thought only of braiding Lali's soft hair. Pain shot through her fingertips–she lightened her touch and kept working. She made one long braid and put it aside.

Her right hand was throbbing, but it hadn't bled again. She tried to rest but couldn't stop. With feet and legs and arms, she gently coaxed the bamboo upward and tied her braided piece around it, about a quarter of the way up. To

make certain it would stay in place, she fastened it to an upward strip of bamboo every few centimeters around. Finding the most level spot on the rug, she set her basket there
and slowly removed her arms.

It stood upright. It stood even.

TWENTY-TWO

My hands couldn't weave, Chong Ata . . . I had to do something else. It's almost a basket . . . or, I think of it as one." Doubt flooded Mehrigul's mind. She hung her head. "At least I didn't spoil the bamboo. It can be used again."

"Why don't you show me what you made, Mehrigul? I'd like to see it."

Mehrigul noticed Ana standing by the door as she reached for the sack that had held the bamboo. She didn't want her to see. Only Chong Ata would pass judgment.

"I would like you to show me, and your ana as well," Chong Ata said. "You would honor her by letting her see what you have done."

Slowly, Mehrigul lowered the sides of the bag.

There it was before her, as tall as the distance between her elbow and the tip of her hand, as wide as her ten fingers at the top. Beautiful narrow strips of bamboo flowing freely upward from a firm base. Mehrigul caught her breath in wonder that her hands had made such a remarkable thing—or so she thought, again, for a fleeting moment. She turned away. She knew you couldn't just gather some bamboo together and call it a basket.

Chong Ata was looking and not saying anything.

"It's not to sell, Chong Ata," she said quickly. "I made it for you. It was just…what the bamboo told me to do."

Chong Ata leaned closer to the object before him. Without touching it, his hands flowed upward with the graceful rise of the bamboo.

Mehrigul waited. Stopped breathing. She'd thought that at least Chong Ata might like it as a present. But there were no tears in his eyes, as there had been before when she showed him her special woven baskets. This time he seemed to be smiling, almost laughing. She closed her eyes, ashamed she'd thought her work might have some worth.

Then Chong Ata spoke. "I would be most pleased to have your basket as a gift, but I want you to show it to the American lady. If she likes it as much as I do, you must let her have it." He sat back, his gaze still fixed on the work before him.

"You like it then, Chong Ata, and I can call it a basket?" She had heard his words, but the meaning hadn't gotten through to her mind. "I shouldn't feel ashamed?"

"Not ashamed, Mehrigul. Proud."

Mehrigul hadn't noticed Ana moving toward them until she knelt at their side.

"I will make a clean cotton bag to carry your basket in," Ana said. "We can wrap it so it will be protected on the way to market."

Mehrigul shot a fierce glance at Ana. She'd spoken of protecting it. But if Ata stormed in and said he wanted it, would she let him have it?

Ana's help was too late. The dirty bag that was cushioning it would do. Mehrigul turned away, only to see Chong Ata shaking his head.

"Thank you, Ana." Mehrigul forced the words through her clamped jaw. Hating that Ana was spoiling her special moment with Chong Ata. Wanting, if only for a brief time, to enjoy the happiness she felt about having a basket to show Mrs. Chazen. She wouldn't have to run away and hide if the American lady really did come back.

"Let me see your hands, Mehrigul," Chong Ata said.

She had already removed the wrapping from her left hand. She held it out, not surprised to see it was still swollen, with reddened blotches.

"And your other hand."

Mehrigul tried not to wince as Chong Ata began to remove the bandage. She looked away and saw Ana's hands cover her eyes. Then Ana quickly rose and disappeared into the house.

By the time Chong Ata had removed all the covering, Ana was back with water and a new paste of crushed herbs. Clean pieces of white cloth hung over her arm. Together, Chong Ata and Ana tended Mehrigul's wounds. Nothing soothed her hands. She steeled herself against the pain, knowing she must have faith in the healing power of the medicine her grandfather spread over her raw flesh.

It was Ana who dressed her hands, using the softest, most precious cotton she had stored away. "I'm sorry, Mehrigul," Ana said. "I should have been in the field helping you. I've not been much use to anyone lately . . . I'm sorry."

Mehrigul knew she should respond, but what could she say? That it didn't matter? That she understood and forgave Ana? Neither was true. She nodded and said nothing.

"If you like . . . I will try to help you bathe . . . and wash your hair," Ana said as she finished tying the bandage. "So you'll be ready . . . for tomorrow."

Almost against her will, Mehrigul let herself be drawn in by Ana's gentle words. "Yes, Ana," she said, the taut muscles in her body softening until she wondered if she could hold herself up. "Thank you."

Maybe the doctor's teas — and learning the truth about Ata — had begun to bring her ana back to them.

Lali, Chong Ata, and Mehrigul ate in peace, kneeling around the platter of rice and peppers that was set before them. Ana brought a treat of freshly made cornmeal-and-onion cakes when she joined them. No one mentioned Ata's absence or the missing donkey and cart. Lali, freed from his grim presence, told stories of her school day.

"My friend taught me a new dance," she said, springing up, her arms above her head moving in wavelike gestures. Then, slowly, she began to circle her wrists, crossing them in graceful arcs, then bending her hands away in lovely curves, all in rhythm to the simple folk tune she sang. Chong Ata clapped in time, and soon Ana joined him. Mehrigul hummed along as she swayed her body.

Now every part of Lali was moving. She turned her neck with little fast shakes. Then bent sideways, backwards, still giving her little shakes. She picked up her skirt and pointed her toe, her legs copying the fast, shivery movements that Uyghur dancers make as she took three steps forward and then slid her foot backwards with a small kick. The more they clapped, the more lively her dance. Chong Ata's head began to tilt and shake.

As Mehrigul got up to dance with her sister, Ata came through the doorway, sucking the music and laughter from the room. Lali ran to hide behind Ana. Mehrigul froze, the shivering in her legs no longer in time to the music.

Ata didn't seem to see them or to have heard them. He moved with heavy gait and slumped beside the eating cloth, his eyes wide in bewilderment, or was it fear?

"What is it?" Mehrigul said, her voice wavering. Something terrible had brought Ata to this state — the Han were taking the farm from them, or he'd heard that Memet was in prison or shot dead.

Ata's mouth worked, but the sound was swallowed inside him. He rocked back and forth.

"What's happened?" Mehrigul pleaded. She was beside Ata, close enough to know there was no stink from wine, which doubled her fears. "Tell us!"

"A message . . . from Memet. He's left Kashgar. I wasn't told how or why. Only that he wouldn't be safe there anymore. He'll cross the Chinese border and go through the mountain pass into Kyrgyzstan. We are to know no more. We can't expect to hear from him . . . maybe . . . for years . . ."

An eerie wail rose from Ana's throat.

"Yes. Cry!" Ata hurled the words at Ana as he lurched to his feet and bolted toward the door. "Our son might as well be dead to us!"

Mehrigul listened to Ana's sobs. To Lali's whimpers as she pulled at Ana's arm.

Silently, Mehrigul got up. She walked out into the yard and crept along the shadows so there would be no chance of meeting Ata. Moved deep into their fields until she was certain she was alone, then fell to her knees. She bowed her head but kept her voice strong.

"Thank you, Allah," she said. "Thank you for keeping Memet safe." He had not been shot or swallowed up by the desert. He had a chance now to begin a new life. Even as she had these thoughts, she wept for the loss of her brother. Maybe forever.

As her cries fell silent, she told her heart the truth she knew. Memet could never return to his life here, at the end of their narrow, poplar-lined lane. He could never bring a young bride here. As much as Memet loved his family and his home, he knew that, too. He had tried to change things and failed.

The chill of the night air enveloped Mehrigul as she looked out at the stark silhouette of leafless trees, a harbinger of the long, cold winter ahead. Fallen leaves scuttled across the field, stirred by the winds blowing from the Taklamakan. The winds that had from time unknown swept over their land, trying to bury them under layers of drifting sand.

The Uyghurs had learned to hold back the desert. It was neither friend nor enemy. But the Han sweeping over their land were nothing like the ebb and flow of drifting sands. The Han had come to stay. And they'd driven Memet away.

And we who are still here — what should we do? Do we have a choice? Mehrigul squeezed her knees against her body, folding herself into a tight ball — against the cold air and the powers that were overwhelming her people. Those who stayed had to do what the cadre ordered. And someone in a far-off place was telling *him* what to do. Someone who didn't like the sound of their beautiful Uyghur language, or the way they lived. Someone who didn't seem to want them here.

Their lives were changing faster and faster. With her whole being, Mehrigul recoiled from the idea of following Memet into an unfamiliar world. She had no yearning to live in a city or to work in a factory. Hadn't Memet warned her? The song haunted her memory. *Don't be taken in, Sister,* he'd sung. *Don't be taken in.*

When the cadre came around with his papers, Mehrigul would have no choice. Ata would sign the lie about her age, and she would be sent thousands of miles away.

Don't be taken in, Sister. Don't be taken in.

Mehrigul couldn't stop the tears that overflowed her eyes. Her tears could flood their whole thirsty oasis, and it wouldn't make any difference or change the way of things.

TWENTY-THREE

THE EASTERN SKY WAS streaked with first light as Mehrigul and Lali stepped outside to gather firewood and fill the kettle. Everything had to go right this morning so Mehrigul and Ata could get a good space at market, one that Mrs. Chazen and Abdul could easily find.

"Hurry, Lali," Mehrigul said, handing her twigs. "Break these into pieces that fit into our stove. That will help Ana."

Lali took a twig and began breaking it at the speed of a snail.

"*Hen kuai de.* Quickly," Mehrigul said, which brought a pout and a great flouncing of shoulders. "No, Lali, you have to help. I can't do it all." Mehrigul's voice was harsh. She turned so Lali wouldn't see the panic in her eyes, the anger at her sister for not moving faster.

Then she dropped her head, forced herself to take in long, deep breaths. "Oh, Lali, it's not you. You know nothing of what's happening. It's important for me to get to market as early as possible. Please do what I ask."

Mehrigul swallowed hard, trying to calm her voice. Lali would only cry and become useless if she was frightened. "Let's hurry now," she said. "Put the pieces on my hands. I'll carry them in, and you can get the water. You're strong. You can lug that by yourself."

When Mehrigul announced that it was time to feed and water the donkey, Lali nodded without protest, and they headed for the shed.

Ata and Chong Ata were seated by the eating cloth when Mehrigul and Lali returned.

"Is that all the naan?" Ata bellowed as Ana laid a few broken pieces on the cloth.

"There are corncakes left from our supper that are for you," Ana said, handing them to him.

Ata grabbed them with a grunt and said no more.

Ana poured tea. They ate in silence. Mehrigul dipped naan into her tea bowl but didn't try to lift the bowl to her lips. She concealed her bandaged hands from Ata as much as possible. He seemed lost in his own world until he finished his cakes. "I see you've fixed the bundles," he said, looking at Mehrigul. "We'll load the cart now."

Mehrigul kept her hands behind her as she braced herself. "I did not prepare the bundles," she said. "Ana did." She paused. "There are only enough for one load."

He threw his arm out. "You'll load the cart then, while I have more tea," he said.

"Mehrigul can't," Ana said, "but I'll do it." She rose slowly from her place at the eating cloth.

Ata jumped up. "What do you mean, she can't?"

"Her hands. They're injured. They . . . they need time to heal," Ana said.

Please don't weaken, Ana, Mehrigul prayed. *Don't back down.* Mehrigul got up and stood beside her. When Lali stood, too, Mehrigul knew it was too much. Their defiance would send Ata into a rage.

She grabbed Lali's hand. "Time for school," Mehrigul whispered as she pulled her sister into the yard. "I know it's early, Lali," she said as they headed for the road. "This morning we'll walk to meet your friends on their way. It was important for us to leave the house."

Every muscle in Mehrigul's legs began to fail her as they moved away. Weak from fear of what could go wrong before they left for market . . . scared of what she'd find when she got back. She had to trust Chong Ata and Ana.

* * *

The donkey cart was hitched and half loaded by the time Mehrigul returned. Ata was doing most of the work, but Ana was helping. Chong Ata kept quiet watch from the yard.

"Change your clothes, Mehrigul," Ana said as she walked by. "Your father will leave soon."

Everything was too calm. Mehrigul changed quickly into her skirt and went to the workroom to get her basket.

It was still there. The cotton strap Ana had sewn onto the bag fit nicely over her arm. With her hands behind her, she could keep it out of Ata's view.

There was no time for words with Chong Ata. For a moment she stopped by his side, his touch filling her with the courage she needed to face a day with so many unknowns.

She headed for the cart, which was loaded high with long cornstalks that covered every inch of the bed and spread wide over the sides.

"You're pretty fancy for walking," Ata said as Mehrigul approached. "But that's what you'll do."

"My legs work," Mehrigul said, then regretted saying it when she saw Ata's eyes narrow to angry slits. She must be careful. Ata wouldn't strike Ana, but Mehrigul could be punished for her disrespect and because Ana had come to her defense. She lowered her head, copying Ana's gesture of compliance. Her bandaged hands and her basket stayed firmly in place at her back.

Without words of leave taking, Ata started toward the road, leading the donkey. Mehrigul turned to nod to Chong Ata and Ana and followed a few paces behind.

Mehrigul hadn't thought how she could make the trip to market without Ata noticing the bag. Riding at the back of the cart, she could have hidden it under her skirt. Today there was no hiding place except behind her back. The powdery gray swirls of dust stirred up by the donkey's hooves and the cart wheels were unbearable, but she couldn't walk in front with Ata. Mehrigul lagged farther behind, hoping Ata would find no reason to talk to her. During their trips to and from market he was usually silent.

A new worry arose as they neared the market. Carts heavy and slow, carrying cut wood for winter fuel, choked the entrance road, piled up in front of them, and soon blocked the road behind them, too. Mehrigul was forced to go to the front of the cart or else be crushed against the cornstalks.

Suddenly, Ata was on the other side of the donkey, next to her, glaring at the bag that hung behind her.

Mehrigul's body tensed. She brought the bag to her side, the side away from Ata. Would he grab it? Smash it?

"Oh, this," she said before he could ask. She must not let him know how desperately she cared.

"Yes. That. What do you have there?" His arm shot out.

"Just . . . something . . . Chong Ata helped with. He thought it would be rude if I didn't have something to bring to the American lady." What she said was not all a lie. She couldn't have made the basket without Chong Ata. With tiny movements Mehrigul tried to ease the bag from Ata's sight, but his eyes stayed glued on it.

He shook his head back and forth. "Do my words have no meaning? I told you to forget about your stupid baskets. Now it's your grandfather. Your mother, too. She helped, didn't she? That's a real pretty cotton bag you have there." He smacked his fist against his leg. Then he closed in, crouching next to Mehrigul until his face almost touched hers. "Show me," he said. "Show me what you've got that's *so* special the whole family had to help you, instead of doing what they're supposed to."

It took all the strength she could summon not to move. Not to run away. She swallowed until she found a voice that could speak over her fear and words that might make him back off. "It's just another of those useless things," she said. "Like before. You would know right away it was worthless, Ata . . . but . . . I was hoping . . . if the lady comes . . . maybe she would give us a few yuan for it."

Ata was still beside her, but he hadn't grabbed the bag. Mehrigul hung her head. "I'm sorry I couldn't help with the cornstalks as you asked me to. I know you wanted to bring a second load. Maybe selling the basket will make up for the money we'll lose today because of that." Mehrigul kept her eyes on the ground. She didn't dare look at Ata's face, but his body seemed to relax. Maybe he was thinking about the hundred yuan. She prayed he wouldn't make her open the bag.

"Well, good luck to you all. Let's hope your fancy lady comes and likes the basket. We need money. Make her pay for the bag, too," he said, and turned his attention to the donkey, jerking his harness, urging him forward in the procession of carts that barely moved.

Ata shuffled ahead a few feet at a time, cursing. Then he began muttering at Mehrigul, who was forced to walk beside him as everyone crowded together at the market entrance. "You're as useless as your brother," he said, "with your stupid basket. You were lucky once. That's all."

TWENTY-FOUR

ATA PARKED THEIR CART at the edge of nowhere. Near the tethered donkeys. Away from fruits and vegetables, cotton and yarn, bags full of colorful spices. In a place Mrs. Chazen would never come to.

"Set the price high," he said as he wandered off.

"When will you be back?" Mehrigul called. Then she clamped her hand over her mouth to keep from screaming. Just once, couldn't he mind the cart and let her go?

Ata shrugged his shoulders in a dismissive gesture and continued a distance down the lane to a spot where men had gathered by a tree.

Mehrigul moved behind the stalks and pulled her scarf over her forehead, knotted it under her chin. It wasn't the same out here. There were a few men around tending carts filled with straw, but no women or girls to whom she might talk. She stayed as hidden as possible, her eyes fixed on Ata.

Osman and another man joined the group. Everyone

stopped talking. Stood tall and formal. *Salams* were exchanged. The man turned and Mehrigul saw his face.

It was the cadre. Led straight to Ata by his friend Osman.

Was this it? The day the papers would be signed and she'd be sent away?

Tears streamed down Mehrigul's face as she stood watching. Her wish had been granted — she'd been given the three weeks' time she'd asked for so she could make a basket and bring it to Mrs. Chazen. That seemed so unimportant now. How could she leave Lali and Chong Ata and Ana? She wanted only to live quietly on their land, even if she was never anything more than a peasant farmer.

As she stared at the group, an uncontrollable burst of laughter welled up from her belly and came out in tiny, choked sounds. For once she might be more valuable to Ata than her brother had been. She might even please him with all the money she'd be sending home.

"Go ahead, Ata. Sign," she hissed through her teeth. She twisted her tongue around in her mouth until she had a good supply of saliva and spit on the ground. That's what Memet would have done.

As she stood watching, the cadre did not single Ata out. Rather quickly, he said his goodbyes to all and walked down the lane, by himself.

Then Ata and Osman and another man were leaving. They followed the same path as the cadre but with no haste in their steps. Ata didn't even give a quick glance back in Mehrigul's direction. Where was he going?

She wanted to yell. Run after him. Make him tell her what was happening. But she didn't. She stayed by the cart, as tethered to it as their donkey to his hitching post. She would be there until Ata decided to return. That was why he had brought her. Wasn't that her duty?

There was little Mehrigul could do but trace the haze-covered sun as it inched across the November sky. And wonder why she should even try to sell cornstalks — or her basket. She covered the white bag that held the basket with her skirt. If the cadre or his wife came around, they didn't need to know about it.

Rather amusing, she thought, but this time no laughter came. Mrs. Chazen and Abdul would have trouble finding her out here in nowhere, but the cadre and his wife would have no problem at all. The local party leader would have little use for her now, though. Ata was the one he needed.

Likely, the teacher had already told the cadre or his wife that Mehrigul had not returned to school.

By noontime, Mehrigul hadn't sold one bundle. More farmers were passing by now. She should try, she knew. Yet all she could manage was to stand behind the cornstalks, her basket hidden under her skirt, and search the lanes. Wondering why she still cared. But she did care, with every inch of her being. What if Mrs. Chazen and Abdul had returned to the market and were looking for her? Even if they couldn't find her right away, they might take an extra minute or two to look for her. She must keep watch.

In time, though, the thought of what Ata would do if she sold nothing took over. A friendly-looking man was coming down the lane. She went to the front of the cart. She remembered how Memet used to call to people when business was slow, telling them they needed radishes, onions, peppers. She'd do that. *Time to feed your donkey,* she'd call out.

No words came.

The words that raged inside Mehrigul were for the way her life had fallen apart, the helplessness she felt against Ata and the world outside that wanted to take her away from all she held dear, and her anger left her silent.

The man passed.

Mehrigul leaned against the cart. Perhaps next time.

A farmer leading a donkey came by. "I'll take two bundles," he said. "Four yuan."

"Ten," she said.

"Four is generous enough," he said, and began to walk away.

"No. Wait. Four is fine . . . if you'll take them from the pile yourself."

The man pulled the yuan from his pocket. He raised his eyebrows as he laid the notes in Mehrigul's bandaged hands. He took the stalks and moved on.

By midafternoon the cart was half empty. Mehrigul had put her basket on the ground by the inside of the cart wheel, where she hoped no one would notice it. She stood at the front of the cart with a bundle of tall stalks at her side, swaying it back and forth to get the attention of passersby. As the sun moved lower in the sky, more and more stopped to buy. She was in the middle of a sale when she caught a flicker of red out of the corner of her eye — a young girl and her mother.

"Just take it. Leave the money," she called as she raced down the lane. "Pati, I'm here!" she shouted, waving her arms as Pati and her mother came around the corner into full view. Shopping bags hung from their arms.

"We've been looking all over for you, Mehrigul. Do you really expect anyone to find you way out here?"

Mehrigul could only shake her head as she struggled to hold back tears, covering her face to hide gasps of relief.

"We saw him — your father," Pati said, "but we didn't want to ask. We just knew you were here somewhere."

Mehrigul found her voice. "Have you seen a foreign lady? She'd be walking around with a Uyghur guide."

Pati and her mother shook their heads. Both put their arms around Mehrigul as she led them back toward the cart.

"I'll stay here so you and Pati can look for her," Pati's mother said.

"I . . . I can't leave. Ata . . ." Mehrigul couldn't go on. He'd be furious. And if he was drunk? "He's not himself since Memet left. I mustn't go."

Pati's mother paused for a moment, studying Mehrigul. "I understand," she said.

"Describe the lady, Mehrigul. We'll find her if she's here," Pati said, her arm still around her friend's shoulder.

"Well, she's different from us. Not Uyghur. Definitely not Chinese. She's a white tourist lady. If you see someone like that, ask if she's Mrs. Chazen. A guide will be with her, named Abdul. He's like our fathers."

"If they're here, we'll find them."

"And, Pati, you know where we usually have our cart? Please tell the people around there where I am. They could tell Abdul. Also the egg woman who sells by the pots and pans. She knows me. She'll help."

Mehrigul tried to be hopeful as she watched Pati and her mother hurry off. Could she be allowed one last dream?

She knew they might return with the news that Mrs. Chazen had already come and gone.

TWENTY-FIVE

Suddenly everyone wanted to buy cornstalks, but Mehrigul didn't want to sell. If Ata came back before Pati and her mother returned and the cart was empty, he'd leave. She'd never know if Mrs. Chazen was looking for her or had come at all. She'd never know if she had made another basket worth one hundred yuan.

Mehrigul put the price for a bundle of cornstalks higher with each sale.

"Four yuan? For one?" a man said. "It's late. Bargain time." He thrust a two-yuan note at her.

"Four," Mehrigul said.

The man pulled out another note, almost threw it at her. "If my donkey could make it home without eating, you'd never get this." He yanked a bundle from the cart.

Then there were only three bundles left.

"Already sold," she told the next farmer, and the next, and the next. "Sold," she said, not looking at them, her eyes fixed only on the pathway to the main market.

Still no Pati or her mother. No Ata. Not even the cadre's wife to bring her news.

"I'll take them all, so you can go home," a man said. He waved a few yuan at her.

Mehrigul backed against the cart. Spread her arms in a protective gesture.

"No . . . no . . . I can't," she stammered.

Then she couldn't go on. She could think only that Pati had not found Mrs. Chazen but hadn't bothered to come back and tell her.

Mehrigul whirled around. Grabbed the bundles with her hands — hard — so it hurt. Heaved them onto the man's cart and grabbed the money. "Take them! Go!" she screamed, and rushed to the back of the cart. She needed to feel the pain — to feel something.

Patches of blood stained the dirty white cotton of her bandages.

She stood beside the white cotton bag that held her basket. The pure whiteness of it shone like a beacon amidst the muted tones of old carts, hard-packed gray earth, the hazed sun that was sinking closer to the crest of the Kunlun.

All that was left out here in nowhere was a girl with a basket.

* * *

Finally, Ata appeared, his gait steady, the same angry, tight expression on his face as always. If he'd signed his daughter's life away, it seemed to have changed nothing. His eyes went to the empty cart — and the bag at Mehrigul's side.

"Couldn't get your hundred yuan, could you? I told you she wouldn't come back."

"Is that all you have to say, Ata? What happened? The cadre?"

Ata didn't answer. He kept moving toward the basket. "Let me see that silly thing no one wants."

Mehrigul grabbed the bag. Skirted around Ata with lightning steps. She would not let him take her basket from her. Not this time.

"I'll buy the mutton," she cried as she fled.

Mehrigul wove in and out among the merchants with no plan, no destination. Stirring up dust. Hoping Pati might still be there. Out of rhythm in this place where the few neighbors left met to chat or bargain in an easygoing way over the price of unsold potatoes.

She slowed when she saw Hajinsa and her mother in front of a table with mutton buns. Hajinsa held a bun to her mouth, nibbling at the bottom and sucking out the fatty broth. Maybe Mehrigul disliked Hajinsa because she always seemed to have enough to eat.

Mehrigul kept close to the table on the opposite side of the path, trying not to be seen. Trying not to think of her own empty stomach. There had been too much else on her mind for her to bother eating the few raisins she had in her pocket.

"Aren't you going to say hello, Mehrigul?" Hajinsa had barely stopped sucking on her bun to call out, her long, thin fingers still holding it close to her mouth, ready to bite into its rich filling.

Mehrigul's mouth watered in spite of herself as she stopped to face Hajinsa. "I guess I didn't see you," she said. "I'm in a hurry. I'm looking for Pati and her mother." She mimicked Hajinsa's arrogant bearing, then wondered why she hadn't just ignored her and moved on.

"We passed them a while ago. They're around." Suddenly, Hajinsa cocked her head. "What are you hiding in the bag behind your back, Mehrigul? Did you actually buy something?"

Hajinsa's mocking tone seared through Mehrigul at the same time she heard Pati's call. "We're here, Mehrigul! We're coming."

Pati was walking toward her with her mother and Mrs. Chazen and Abdul.

TWENTY-SIX

MEHRIGUL STOOD PARALYZED, AS if watching a mirage in the desert. *If I shut my eyes,* she told herself, *no one will be there when I open them.*

She closed and opened her eyes. Mrs. Chazen was walking toward her, wearing the same wide-brimmed hat as the time before, the same comfortable shoes. Slowly, Mehrigul brought her arm from behind her back and held the white bag in front of her.

"We almost gave up trying to find you," Abdul said. "When you were not in the same spot, we had no idea where to look."

"You've found her now, and what she has for you is very special," Pati said, moving over to stand beside her friend.

Mehrigul pulled in a quick breath. Pati didn't know. She'd only seen the grapevine baskets, before Ata took them — not one made from bamboo.

The bamboo basket was not what Mrs. Chazen expected. What if she didn't like it? Thank you, she'd say, but no one in my shop would want it. And walk away.

They were standing around Mehrigul, waiting.

The English words she'd practiced were trapped in her throat. She swallowed, afraid to let them out. But it wasn't the words she was afraid of — it was the answer.

"I have one basket, Mrs. Chazen," Mehrigul said, her English words slow and without music, and started to open the bag. Then she turned to Abdul and poured out words in Uyghur. "I made more that Mrs. Chazen might have liked better, but I don't have them now. They're gone. I know I can do it again . . . if I have time . . . if the American lady is able to come back."

Abdul gave a nod and turned to Mrs. Chazen. For a moment they spoke in English.

"It is unlikely she will come back anytime soon, Mehrigul. Perhaps in a few years. But she would like to see what it is you have brought," Abdul said.

With shaky hands, Mehrigul placed the bag on the ground. She caught a glimpse of Hajinsa, a smirk on her face as she stood watching, amused at Mehrigul's distress.

All Mehrigul wanted to do was run away. No one here needed to see her basket. It was Chong Ata's gift. Hadn't she given it to him? But Chong Ata had said she must first show her basket to the American lady. Mehrigul must let her have it, if she liked it.

Mehrigul knelt beside the cotton bag. There was a stain of blood on the handle where she'd grabbed it. She was extra careful as she pulled away the protective coverings and cupped the base of the basket with her bandaged hands. As she touched the bamboo, she thought of the cloth she had tied to the culm, the token that carried her wish — to make something of beauty that would help her family. She asked, again, for her wish to be granted.

Lifting her basket from its coverings, she set it upright on the bag.

The creamy yellow color of Chong Ata's bamboo, flowing upright and free, was even more lovely than Mehrigul remembered. No matter what happened — no matter what her life would have to be — she would find time to keep making baskets. And, Allah willing, Chong Ata would not yet have lived out his days, and would be there to teach her how to craft baskets from all their land's riches when she returned.

No one was saying anything. Mehrigul knew she must look up. She was ready, now, to know what Mrs. Chazen thought.

She rocked back on her haunches, preparing to stand, when suddenly Mrs. Chazen squatted on the other side of the basket, right there on the dusty pathway.

"Mehrigul," she said, studying first the basket, then Mehrigul's face, back and forth, back and forth. She opened her mouth to speak, then turned to Abdul and let out a string of English words.

Abdul squatted beside them. "She wants me to tell you that you have made an unusual basket, a remarkable one, that she would be privileged to have for her own. It is so much more than she expected."

Heat rose in Mehrigul's face. Her heart beat too fast. She folded her hands to still her excitement.

"Please thank Mrs. Chazen," she said quietly. "But there is something she needs to know. I could not have made the basket if it hadn't been for my grandfather. It was he who prepared the bamboo. He gave it to me, and I tried to do something with it that wouldn't spoil its beauty. So, you see" — she looked up now, her eyes meeting Mrs. Chazen's, wishing she had her own English words — "it's really my grandfather's basket."

Mehrigul watched as Mrs. Chazen listened to Abdul. She could not guess what the American lady was thinking.

Finally, Mrs. Chazen nodded and gave her reply.

"Mrs. Chazen believes," Abdul said, "that your grandfather is a very good artisan and there is much you can learn from him. But that you, Mehrigul, have an unusual creative strength that is all your own, and you must take credit."

As she fought to absorb these words, to believe they were meant for her, she saw Mrs. Chazen reach into her bag. She would ask how much Mehrigul wanted for her basket. Could she say one hundred yuan out loud, for everyone to hear? It was the first time she'd remembered that others were watching and listening.

Mehrigul's eyes went to Hajinsa, who stood gawking, the half-eaten mutton bun still in her hand. Pati and her mother were arm in arm, smiling, nodding their heads when they caught Mehrigul's glance.

"Mrs. Chazen would like to pay you," Abdul said. "She wonders if two thousand yuan would be acceptable?"

"How . . . much?" Mehrigul asked. She knew she'd heard wrong. That was more than half of what they made all year!

"Two thousand yuan! Wow!" Pati let out before clapping her hand over her mouth.

Laughing, Mrs. Chazen and Abdul stood up. Mehrigul stayed squatting, not at all sure what she should do.

Mrs. Chazen reached toward Mehrigul, then stopped and pointed to Mehrigul's bandaged hands, her head tilted in question.

"Are your hands injured badly, Mehrigul?" Abdul asked.

"No." She shook her head, hoping they hadn't seen the bloodstains. "I've been working in the fields. It's time to plant winter wheat. I'm not used to that kind of work."

"Aren't you still in school, Mehrigul?" Abdul asked.

Slowly, Mehrigul stood. Lowered her eyes. Unwilling to speak the truth in front of Hajinsa.

When she did not answer, Mrs. Chazen put her hand on Abdul's arm. They spoke for a long time.

"Is your family here with you? Mrs. Chazen and I would like to meet them," Abdul said.

"My ata," Mehrigul said.

"Would you like Pati and me to go with you?" Pati's mother asked.

There was comfort in her words, but Mehrigul knew that whatever happened must be between her and her father. He would be angry enough when he heard they knew about the money. And she had to tell him herself.

"Thank you for all you've already done. I'll be fine."

Pati and her mother gave her a hug and left, Hajinsa

and her mother trailing behind them. Mehrigul put her basket back into the cotton bag and, with Abdul and Mrs. Chazen, walked in the opposite direction.

After a few steps, Mehrigul turned and looked over her shoulder. Her eyes met Hajinsa's, staring back at her. Hajinsa turned away. Mehrigul walked taller, her worth no longer defined by the way she chose to tie her headscarf.

TWENTY-SEVEN

MEHRIGUL TOLD HER STORY as she and Mrs. Chazen and Abdul wove their way along the paths, half empty now that the market day was coming to a close. She spoke of Memet's leaving and of her own childish hope that she could stay with the land that had been her grandfather's, their family's for hundreds of years. She said little about her father, for she didn't know what to say or if he'd even be there waiting. She did not speak of the cadre's plans for her.

Abdul and Mrs. Chazen exchanged many words of English. The scowl on Mrs. Chazen's face worried Mehrigul. She could not guess its meaning.

When they came to the place where hay and straw were sold, Ata was alone behind their empty cart, watching them approach. His arms folded across his chest. He stood stiff and hard-faced. His eyes narrowed, shifting between Mrs. Chazen and Abdul. He didn't look at Mehrigul.

"*Assalam alaykum,*" Abdul said, his hand rising to his chest, palm open, bowing.

Ata lowered one arm and kept the other tight to his chest, his fist clenched. *"Wa alaykum assalam,"* he replied, his head barely inclined. Mehrigul cringed at his rudeness.

"I am here with Mrs. Chazen, from the United States," Abdul said. "She admires your daughter's work, especially the bamboo basket she brought today. She has offered a very generous amount for its purchase."

A look of confusion passed briefly over Ata's face. He had been expecting a grapevine basket, Mehrigul knew. Then he again steeled his expression.

There was an awkward silence as Abdul waited for Ata's response.

Finally, Ata shrugged. "I see no problem," he said. "I'm certain we can settle on a price."

Mehrigul dropped her head, embarrassed at the swagger that had crept into Ata's voice.

To her relief, Abdul raised his hand, stopping Ata from saying more. "Mrs. Chazen has already named an amount to Mehrigul. I believe you will be quite satisfied. She would like to offer —"

"I know what the American lady paid for the grapevine basket," Ata said, the fingers of one hand brushing at his beard, while he cocked his other hand at his waist. "Think what one made from bamboo might cost!"

Mehrigul could bear no more. "No, Ata!" She ran to his side. "Don't!" Her whole body contorted in shame for him.

Ata's elbow swung out to shove Mehrigul aside. Abdul stepped closer and Ata froze.

"Please let me speak," Abdul said, his voice firm. "Mrs. Chazen has offered Mehrigul two thousand yuan for her basket."

Ata lurched back. "For her basket?" His head was shaking in that awful way that was half laughter and half disbelief.

Then, slowly, Ata turned to glare at Mrs. Chazen, and Mehrigul remembered his words: *What else does she want from you?* Why couldn't Ata trust Abdul and Mrs. Chazen? Why was he acting like this?

"It is a generous sum," Abdul said, "and there could be more. Mrs. Chazen is interested in making a long-term arrangement with Mehrigul to supply baskets for her shop."

"No one pays that much for baskets," Ata said.

"Has your father not seen your work, Mehrigul?"

A chill crept over her body as she heard Abdul's question. She looked at the bag clutched to her side, the bag that covered her betrayal of her father — a basket she had been forbidden to make. She did not want him to see it.

She shook her head slightly without looking up.

"Perhaps you should show him, so he'll understand its worth."

As she stooped and uncovered her basket, Abdul and Mrs. Chazen were speaking in English. Quietly at first, then Mrs. Chazen's words were louder, sharper. Fear gripped Mehrigul — fear that now Mrs. Chazen had seen the basket again, she no longer wanted it.

Mehrigul forced herself to raise her eyes. Mrs. Chazen was staring at Ata, not her. At Ata, who thrust out his arm, pointing at the basket.

"What is that thing?" he said. He looked flustered as he moved toward Mehrigul. "It's not even a basket. It couldn't be worth that much."

Mehrigul rose and stood in front of her work. Abdul went to her side.

"Please don't misunderstand," he said. "Mrs. Chazen is honorable. I have helped her acquire crafts from our townships for many years. Your daughter's work is more than just a basket; it is an unusual work of art. Mrs. Chazen believes it will sell very successfully in her shop in America."

Ata stood ill at ease, his eyes darting back and forth between Abdul and Mrs. Chazen.

"Mrs. Chazen has helped many of our Uyghur people," Abdul said. "She buys their handmade felt rugs, their wooden bowls, their handwoven ikat silks. She knows well the value of Mehrigul's basket."

Mehrigul listened to Abdul's words in wonder, awed that she might be thought of in the same way as these respected craftsmen. For the first time in uncountable days, Mehrigul allowed herself gladness, a feeling that began to ease the tight bands behind her eyes. Could she believe again that there was good in the world — someone who didn't want to harm them but to help? Could Ata believe that?

"These are difficult times." Abdul spoke solemnly to Ata. "I have two daughters. I worry about their future. It's hard to know what tomorrow will bring for them. Or for us." He paused. "You are very fortunate. Mehrigul has a special talent. She can have a good future. Mrs. Chazen and I, too, want to help her. To help you." Abdul studied Ata's face for a moment. "We must recognize goodwill when it's offered."

Ata turned his head fiercely — away from Abdul. Then, slowly, his shoulders slumped and his clasped hands hung in front of him. Now Mehrigul knew that the cadre had talked to him. Ata was thinking of what the future would bring for his daughter.

"I know, Ata," Mehrigul said. "The cadre's wife has talked to me. I know my name is on the list."

She turned to Mrs. Chazen. "Please," she said. "Please tell Mrs. Chazen how much I want to make more baskets for her. How grateful I am that she wants them. Only . . . I can't . . . I won't be able to." Tears flooded Mehrigul's eyes, but she couldn't tell if they fell to her cheeks. There was no feeling left in her body. She wondered how she was still standing, yet she went on, directing her words to Abdul now. "Because I no longer go to school, I have been selected to be sent to the south of China to work in a factory. It won't be possible for me to make more baskets."

There was silence for a moment as Mrs. Chazen turned to Abdul, wondering what had been said. Abdul held his finger to his lips.

The longer Abdul stood silent, the more uneasy Ata became. "I couldn't let Mehrigul go to school," he said finally, his voice rising. "My son left us. Her mother's . . . sick." His face twisted and he threw his arms wide. "She had to work on the farm. She was all the help I had. She couldn't go to school and do that too."

"I'm sorry to hear your son left," Abdul said after a pause. "That must be very hard for you. You're fortunate, though, to have a gifted daughter who will be able to help you in other ways." Again he paused. "Is it certain that Mehrigul must go?"

"I haven't signed the papers. I am to be at the local party leader's office next week."

"Ata," Mehrigul whispered. Words she hadn't dared even to think before were forming in her head. She was going to say them to Ata, no matter what might happen.

"If you let me go back to school, maybe you won't have to sign." Her lips trembled, but she let the words tumble out before they got smothered inside. "You see . . . Ata . . . I would like to go back to school . . . and have time to make baskets." Mehrigul lifted her head and looked directly at him. Looked at him and would not turn away. "Please. That's what I would like to do. Maybe some of the money from the basket could be used to hire help for you this winter."

Had Ata heard her? His face showed no response, but his eyes were black and bitter and cold. She knew she had been disrespectful to say so much. Her better sense told her to bow her head and fold her hands, but her arms would not move, her head would not bend.

Mehrigul gasped with relief when Ata finally turned away to look at Abdul, who was speaking quietly to Mrs. Chazen. Then, too quickly, everyone was looking at her again, and she knew she must stand as sturdy as the desert tamarisk, as steadfast as Chong Ata. She was surprised at the courage that brought her. "I told the cadre's wife I expected to go back to school at the end of harvest," Mehrigul said to Ata. "We've gathered our summer crops. The winter wheat is planted. Maybe . . . if I go back now . . ."

Ata flailed his arms. "It's too late. I've said I'd sign. The cadre won't like it if I change my mind. They have their quota to fill." He began to pace back and forth, stamping his feet. "I may have to pay him or give up more of our land if you don't go. They look for any excuse."

"I know what you say is true," Abdul said, his voice gentle and calming. He walked quietly at Ata's side until Ata's steps slowed and finally stopped. "How old is your daughter?"

"I'm four —" Mehrigul felt a tap on her wrist. With her arm around Mehrigul, Mrs. Chazen led her aside.

"Fourteen," Ata said, with a cold glance at Mehrigul.

Mehrigul regretted that she'd tried to answer. She'd already said more than she should have. Perhaps Mrs. Chazen understood this and was telling her to let the men talk. Strangely, Mehrigul felt comforted and strong as she stood beside Mrs. Chazen.

Again Abdul spoke in his gentle, quiet voice. "If you haven't signed, and Mehrigul goes to school immediately, the cadre might reverse his demand or agree to a delay until she is of age, at sixteen."

"He'll want something from me to make that happen. I know." Ata spit the words out. "We're treated like scum in our own country."

Abdul put his hand on Ata's arm. "I know your cadre," he said. "We grew up together in a township not far from here. He has become a bitter man, working against the will of his own people. I will go with you. We'll meet with him together. If you agree to follow the rules—if Mehrigul stays in school—he should be obliged to change his order." Abdul hesitated. "You could offer him a small gift."

Abdul gave a quick, reassuring look at Mehrigul before turning again to Ata. "I will offer my guarantee to the cadre that this agreement will be kept."

Ata's eyes flashed wariness, but the heat of his anger seemed to have passed. "Perhaps something can be worked out," he said to Abdul, his glance never once going to Mehrigul. "The meeting is next Monday at two o'clock."

"I'll help in any way I can," Abdul said, and Ata nodded.

Abdul turned to Mrs. Chazen, explaining in English what had taken place.

Then Mrs. Chazen was counting out yuan notes into Abdul's hands. Mehrigul's own hands flew to her mouth to stifle her protest as Abdul handed the notes to Ata. Ata's brows arched in disbelief as he reached to accept them. The black hardness of his eyes had not softened. Mehrigul saw no good reason to believe that Ata might change — that he would not think it all right to spend the money on gambling and wine.

"If everything works out," Abdul was saying, "Mrs. Chazen wants very much for Mehrigul to make more baskets. If you and Mehrigul agree, I'll come to your farm once a month and pay a hundred yuan for each vine basket Mehrigul makes. Of course, there will be more for baskets that are as unique and wonderful as the one she brought to us today."

Mehrigul looked at her hands. Hands that a few days ago had lost their talent for making even a simple vine basket. Only the magic of Chong Ata's bamboo had rescued her.

Mehrigul stole a shy glance at Mrs. Chazen. Mrs. Chazen was looking at her with the same reassuring smile she remembered from before. She lowered her head, not knowing how to respond. But she knew with all her heart that she could make more baskets. She must. And she would.

As Abdul and Ata kept talking, Mehrigul again felt a touch on her arm. Mrs. Chazen was beside her with the camera, gesturing for Mehrigul to hold the basket. She lifted it and tried to force her lips into a pleasant expression, but her mind stirred with too many unknowns for her to give in to the happiness she wanted to feel. She felt self-conscious and scared as the camera kept flashing, over and over again.

Then Abdul had the camera and was taking pictures of Mehrigul and Mrs. Chazen together.

And then Abdul and Mrs. Chazen walked away, down the path, the white bag dangling from the American lady's arm.

TWENTY-EIGHT

MEHRIGUL STOOD ALONE WITH Ata, watching Mrs. Chazen and Abdul until they disappeared around the corner at the end of the nearly empty pathway.

Was it possible that she might not have to leave? How hard would Ata plead with the cadre to take her name off the list? He could keep the two thousand yuan and still agree to have her sent away. If he could please the local leader and get the money she'd earn at a factory, he might think that a better arrangement.

"There's something you must know, Ata," Mehrigul said. She kept her eyes on the dusty ground. She didn't want to look at him, to see the storm that would flash across his face. "I wasn't alone when I met the American lady. Pati and her mother were there ... and others."

The silence that was his answer was worse.

"They saw my basket ... and know about the yuan," she blurted out. Money was earned in the marketplace by men, not their wives or daughters, even though they helped to sell. Word of Mehrigul's exchange would spread to Ata's friends, and there was nothing she could do about it. She hadn't planned it that way.

Again, Ata made no reply.

A new feeling filled Mehrigul. A stubbornness she couldn't control. She would not look at him — if that was what he was waiting for. "I never got to buy the mutton," she said. "I'll go now. I have money from the cornstalks." Mehrigul turned to leave.

"No," Ata said, stopping her. "I'll go." He set off, his stride long, steady with purpose.

Mehrigul's heart sank as she watched him disappear. She might better have made him say something, endured his abuse, instead of letting him walk away. Surely, he'd find some way to get a drink, and maybe, if he was lucky, men were still huddled around the gambling table. He'd begin the celebration of her good fortune with wine and gambling.

She wished she'd never made the basket!

Her eyes blurred with tears, she stumbled toward the cart and sat crouched against the triangular crossbar at its head, the triangle of wood where she and Memet had tied the vine-woven cornucopia that started it all.

Here she sat, the "gifted daughter," Abdul had called

her. Which had made her believe there might be some hope for her and her family. Only if the two thousand yuan Ata had in his pocket was carefully spent. "Go back to school . . . make more baskets." Another foolish dream.

Mehrigul slid from the cart. Paced back and forth in the lane, trying not to think of what would happen next.

The visit from Mrs. Chazen was so unreal. Her hands so empty now.

Then Ata was coming toward her, leading the donkey. He was carrying two packages and thrust one at her. "Open it," he said, his head turned away. He laid the other packet on the cart and went about putting the shafts through the loops on the donkey's belly band and into the collar.

She could only keep staring through the clear plastic bag at something that was the shade of the early-evening sky. Something patterned with traces of turquoise and black. Mehrigul lifted it from the package. Rubbed a corner against her face and felt the softest silk she had ever known. It was a scarf she could never wear. It was much too lovely.

A few steps closer to Ata, she found her voice. "Thank you," she said. "It's beautiful."

He kept on working, his back to her.

Mehrigul walked to the rear of the cart, prepared to hop

on when Ata was ready to go. The smell from the other package reached her nostrils. It was the sharp, biting odor of raw mutton — a much bigger package than she and Memet had ever bought. Her stomach grumbled at the thought of the rich meat that would be tonight's supper. At least tonight her family would feast on the money she'd made.

Mehrigul swung herself onto the cart as it pulled away. Maybe in the peacefulness of their country lane she would come to know the meaning of what Ata had just done. The scarf was the only gift he had ever given her, and he'd bought it with her money! Was that the thanks she'd get for earning two thousand yuan?

Maybe Ata had figured out he'd have even more money if he sent her away, and the scarf was meant to make up for it.

Mehrigul's body rocked to the steady rhythm of the turning wheels as she stared back at the vanishing marketplace. Her eyelids, heavy with weariness and her whirling thoughts, began to close. Again she saw Mrs. Chazen and Abdul, Mrs. Chazen with a white bag dangling from her arm. They were walking down the path. Away from her. Getting smaller and smaller and smaller, until they were tiny specks. Mehrigul strained to keep the picture in her mind until she sank onto the wooden planks in a fitful sleep.

TWENTY-NINE

LALI'S CRIES WOKE MEHRIGUL. Lali was jumping up and down in the yard, waving, running circles around Ana as they watched Ata and Mehrigul make their way down the poplar-lined road toward home. For a moment, the joy of selling her basket — of hearing such wonderful words of praise — overcame Mehrigul. She yearned to leap from the cart and rush to greet them, but she held back. Ata must be the one to tell the story of the two thousand yuan, if he chose to. And of his meeting with the cadre.

Mehrigul shivered. An evening chill had crept in as the sun dipped behind the Kunlun, but she wasn't certain if she trembled from the cold.

Lali broke loose from Ana's hold and ran down the road. Mehrigul slid off the cart. Held the soft goodness of Lali tight to her, until Lali wiggled free and pulled her down so she could whisper.

"Na wei nushi xihuan ni de Lanzi ma?" Lali said. "Did the lady like your basket?"

Mehrigul flinched at the sounds of the Mandarin. "Let's only speak our beautiful Uyghur tonight. Our secret language can wait for another day," she said. "You see, this is a very special occasion. The lady did like my basket." She gave Lali another hug.

"Lali, there's a package for Ana on the cart. You run along. Take it to her right away. Then you must help her. Do whatever she tells you." Mehrigul rubbed her belly and licked her lips, and Lali did the same. "Go," Mehrigul said, pushing Lali on her way.

Surely Ana would guess that the day had been a success. She would notice that the white cotton bag she'd made for Mehrigul no longer swung from her arm.

It was hard to stay at Ata's side. There was nothing to be done with the cart that he couldn't do by himself, but Mehrigul knew she couldn't run ahead. Whatever version of the story was told, it had to be Ata's.

They both walked beside the cart, heading around the back of the house toward the shed. In spite of the pain in her hands, Mehrigul raked dirty straw from the shed and carried in fresh. As Ata was releasing the donkey from the harness, she took the bucket to get water from the spigot.

"Mehrigul?" a quiet voice called as she headed back to the shed.

"Chong Ata?" He was by the door of his workroom, squatting in the darkness. "Oh, Chong Ata." She dropped the pail and ran to him. Squatted beside him. "The American lady loved our basket. She thought it very valuable. Because of the bamboo."

"No, Granddaughter, because of what you did with it. Anyone can prepare bamboo."

Mehrigul put her hands over Chong Ata's as they rested on his knees. "You must teach me how. I want to learn everything your father taught you. Weaving is not enough to know. And we will somehow gather tamarisk from the desert. Only you, Chong Ata, can teach me how to weave the spirit of our people into a basket."

"That cannot be taught, Mehrigul, but it is something you already know. I saw it in your basket. Still, there will be much for you to learn. Come spring . . ." He paused. His head fell to his chest as he looked away. "There will be much we can do," he said in a voice Mehrigul could hardly hear.

She heard and could only think of the love and wisdom she must leave behind if forced to go. Or . . . that Chong Ata might leave her even if she wasn't sent away. "I hope, Chong Ata, that we — that you — will have a good, warm

winter, so we can get to our work when spring arrives."
Mehrigul urged him to his feet. "Come," she said, "you go
inside. I'll take the pail to Ata."

Mehrigul was thankful for the darkness that swallowed the lingering traces of daylight. It hid the moisture
that clouded her eyes.

Ata did not ask what had taken her so long. He took
the pail and put it in front of the donkey, now roped inside
the shed. He had gathered the twigs they needed for the
night. They each picked up a bundle and headed for the
house.

By the time they had laid the twigs at the door, Ana
was beside them. She had a basin in one hand. In the other
she held a copper pitcher. She gestured to Ata to hold his
hands over the basin.

For a moment, Ata stood stiffly beside her. Slowly, as
if lifting heavy weights, he raised his hands. Mehrigul
wondered why he was resisting this return to their long-
abandoned ritual. A practice that seemed to have no place
in these times — primitive, Chinese officials called it. They
feared the customs the Uyghurs clung to. Was Ata afraid
they might get caught and punished?

He held his hands steady while Ana poured water

over them. He rubbed his hands together. Twice more the ritual was repeated. As was the custom, Ata did not shake his hands dry; that would have been impolite and unlucky. He waited until Lali, who stood beside Ana, offered him a towel. He used it and returned it to her.

Ata's black eyebrows were still pinched together, suggesting some kind of lingering distrust or anger, as he went inside the house. With the yuan in his pocket, couldn't he allow himself a few moments of contentment with his family?

Mehrigul's legs almost collapsed under her as her thoughts overwhelmed her. He still *had* the yuan, didn't he? He'd left her, gone off into the market. What if he'd owed money . . . maybe to people like Osman? And had already paid it off?

Mehrigul barely felt Lali take her arm and lead her to the ritual bowl. She knew she must not let her fears disturb the sanctity of the honor Ana was bestowing upon her. She held up her hands. Three times Ana sprinkled water over the bandages. Three times Mehrigul rubbed her hands and tried to let the power of the ritual washing calm her. Lali lifted the towel and gently patted the wet cotton, then walked with Mehrigul to the eating cloth and helped her to sit at Chong Ata's side.

"Lali, come, bring tea to your ata and Mehrigul. They've had a busy day at market." Ana was already at the kitchen ledge, pouring tea into bowls.

The tea was set in front of them in a most solemn way. Lali had never tried so hard to please. Mehrigul forced her lips into a straight line to keep from smiling. For a moment she let the warmth and tenderness she felt for Lali and Chong Ata, and even for Ana, overcome her fears. Hard times had weighed down the family for years. Their survival had only lately become Mehrigul's burden, too. Perhaps she understood more now.

As she reached to cup her hands around the tea bowl, to feel its warmth, Mehrigul saw that everyone was looking at her. She lowered her head. "Ata?" she said.

"Perhaps Mehrigul would like me to tell her news," he said.

Mehrigul pulled her hands back. Folded them in her lap. She hated the mocking way he'd said the words. She didn't know what to expect, but Ata knew he'd have to say something, at least about the money. Pati and her mother knew.

She heard Ana catch her breath. When she looked up, Ata was silently laying out money on the eating cloth. One-hundred-yuan notes. There were twenty of them. Ata had not spent her money for the mutton, or for her scarf.

"The American lady paid a high price for Mehrigul's basket," Ata said. "There is an arrangement for her to buy more, if Mehrigul is not —"

"My sister's famous," Lali said, her eyes growing wider and wider.

"I was very lucky, Lali, that someone saw my basket and really wanted it." Mehrigul beckoned to her sister. "Come, sit next to me. I haven't changed one bit."

With Lali nestled close, Mehrigul looked again at Ata. What was he about to say when Lali interrupted? He sat hunched over, his hands in front of him. Again and again he pressed his thumb into his palm.

"The man with the American lady was Uyghur," Ata said, fixing his eyes on the yuan. "His name is Abdul Khalil. He grew up in a nearby township and now lives in Hotan, where he works as a guide." He paused. "I trust him.

"He...ah..." Ata dropped his head, his chin tight to his chest, his hands pressing nervously up and down his thighs. "He thought Mehrigul might go back to school — if she'd be foolish enough to want to waste her time doing that."

No! I said it, Ata. I want to go back to school. Is it foolish to want to give myself some chance of making a life here, with my own people? Is it foolish to not want to be sent away to work in a factory? The words screamed in Mehrigul's head, but only a gasp escaped from her mouth.

If Ata heard, he did not show it.

Silence hung over the room, as if no one dared breathe. Lali's eyes were shifting uneasily from Mehrigul to her ata, and Ana's hand crept to Lali's arm to still her.

Slowly at first, then more rapidly, Ata's body pitched back and forth, his mouth tightly drawn, holding back words Mehrigul could not guess at.

With a suddenness that caught her off-guard, Ata turned to her, his eyes fierce, piercing. "Could you do that? Go to school and have time to make more baskets?"

"Yes . . . Ata . . . I think I can." Mehrigul's voice trembled. Why was he so angry when he asked that question? She forced herself to keep a steady gaze.

And then she understood. Ata wasn't angry. He was afraid. Frightened that Mehrigul might fail. If she did, everything would be lost, for all of them. Ata had given up all hope when Memet left. He was afraid to hope again, to believe his family had been given another chance.

Mehrigul now had some trust that her ata might fight

for her to stay home with her family. And, with Abdul's support, that might be allowed to happen.

She softened her face. Placed her hands on her heart. "Yes, Ata," Mehrigul said. "With everyone's help, I will be able to make baskets that someone wants to buy." She wanted to, with all her being. She was proud to be the one chosen to carry on the family's tradition. Chong Ata's tradition. Silently, she asked again that the wish on her token be granted. To let her hands make beautiful work, and to give her the strength to carry on.

She would find a new secret place and tie another piece of cloth to a stem that reached for the sky. This time, she would ask for God's help in letting her baskets tell the story of her people's desire to be free. Each would carry that hidden message in the flow of the vines and branches. Some would be bright and colorful with scraps of Pati's felt, to show the true nature of their Uyghur hearts. They would all have a meaning that the Han would never understand or try to destroy with a gun.

Maybe those who liked and bought her baskets would somehow know.

Everyone was watching her again. Mehrigul was not used to being the center of attention. Ill at ease, she pressed her arms against her sides. She felt her package, the gift from Ata she'd kept in her pocket. She took it out and held it up for everyone to see.

"Ata gave this to me," she said.

"Oh, it's pretty," Lali said, pulling at an end, feeling it with her fingers. "And so soft."

Ana rose and went to Mehrigul. She removed the old scarf and reached for the new one, tying it loosely in back so the fullness of Mehrigul's jet-black hair framed her face. "It is lovely," Ana said.

Again there was an awkward silence in a family that had grown unused to sharing more than the basic needs of survival.

Until Ata spoke, asking Lali to bring him the *rawap*.

For a moment he just held the instrument across his chest, cradling it in his arms. Slowly, his right hand moved across the small, bowl-shaped body, plucking strings that had fallen out of tune from many weeks of neglect. Ata slid his other hand over the long neck to the tuning pegs, leaning his ear close to the strings as he adjusted the pitches. Soft, mournful chords began to fill the room.

Mehrigul closed her eyes and tried to bring back a memory from long ago, when her uncle and aunt, their family, relatives, and neighbors sat outside their house at harvest time, playing instruments, dancing, singing — before they had been driven away by hard times and distant promises of a better life. There had been sad songs, but there had been lively ones, too.

So very long ago.

The sounds Ata made on the *rawap* now were filled with grief. Sounds that told what lay in his heart unsaid.

Then a melody began to emerge from the chords. One Mehrigul knew. A song Memet had heard in the cafés in Hotan, and played and sung for them:

> *When a tree is covered with ripe fruit it bows down*
> *Don't be proud*
> *Those who stand tall and bear no fruit take the*
>   *fruit of others*
> *Don't be proud*

Ata stopped singing. Only his fingers moved, repeating the chord he had stopped on over and over. Creating sounds that wept for him, and with him. Wept for the oppression of his people.

"No, Ata," Mehrigul said. "We can't let them take from us what is ours. Our soft hearts must not betray our spirits." She lowered her eyes. Maybe she'd said more than was her place, but she had no urge to take back her words.

"Let's finish the song," she said.

Ata stopped strumming. "Don't be proud," Mehrigul whispered. "Don't be proud."

Finally, Ata nodded. He took a firmer grip on the *rawap*. A different swell of notes sounded — the lead into the next line.

> *We live our lives unequal but in the grave all are the*
> *same dust . . .*

Mehrigul sang along in a quiet voice. If she was given a chance, here in their own land beside the desert in the shadow of the mountains, she would make herself heard.

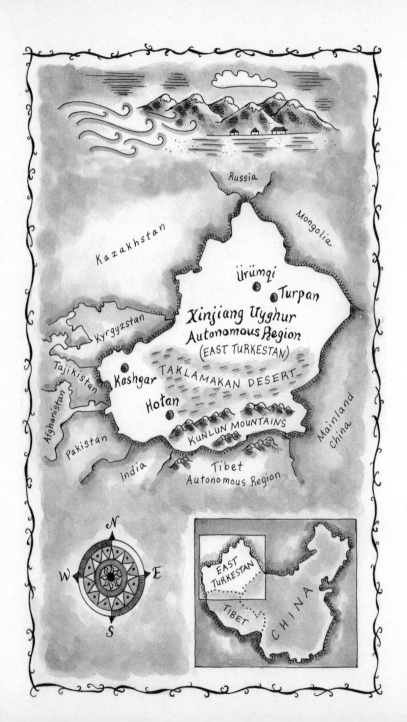

A NOTE FROM MAMATJAN JUMA,
UYGHUR SERVICE EDITOR, RADIO FREE ASIA

I read *The Vine Basket* with joy and tears. I loved it.

The story takes place in a small community on the edge of the Taklamakan Desert in East Turkestan's (Xinjiang Uyghur Autonomous Region's) Hotan prefecture. I grew up in a similar village. Life was simpler and happier then, when my Uyghur culture was dominant in the region. Still, I was filled with nostalgia when I read this book. I strongly recommend it for those who want to learn about what life is like in the lesser-known parts of China.

The Vine Basket touches on many aspects of the Uyghur political situation. It describes the experiences of a teenage girl struggling to find her way in a world where Uyghurs trying to live a traditional lifestyle are prohibited from doing so because of the Chinese government's repressive cultural and ethnic policies. Many observers feel that Uyghur identity, culture, language, and religion are in danger of being lost forever. This book could almost be read as a handbook for young Uyghurs dealing with the pressures of modern society in East Turkestan.

The author's care and hard work have given us a story that has never been told before. I am personally indebted to her for telling it so well.

AUTHOR'S NOTE

The Uyghur people live in a region of the People's Republic of China called Xinjiang. The Uyghurs call it East Turkestan. I have traveled there, to the ancient city of Hotan, which lies along the path of the old Silk Road at the southern edge of the vast Taklamakan Desert. The wind from that desert blew sand and dirt into my face and pummeled the building where I stayed until, at last, a miraculous rain fell to clear the air and refresh the land. I visited the surrounding countryside and watched corn being ground between two huge stones at the grist mill and walked beside the millstream. I purchased a hard-boiled egg at the local market. What I remember most is a young Uyghur girl who offered me a peach from her family's orchard as I stood with my guide watching her grandfather weave a willow basket in the front yard of their home.

Sometime later I learned that Uyghur girls were being forced to work in Chinese factories far from their homes and families, that local cadres had quotas to fill and that the girls were given no choice. This was a story I wanted to tell. The young peasant girl who had offered me a peach became Mehrigul, and I imagined what her life might be.

The Uyghur people are distinct from the Chinese. Their physical appearance, their language and customs, and their Muslim religion are more like those of the Turkic peoples of Central Asia, in countries such as Kyrgyzstan and Tajikistan, than those of the Chinese. The Uyghurs established their own country and their own identity two thousand five hundred years ago. Though their Islamic identity can be traced to A.D. 934, when the city of Kashgar became one of the major learning centers of Islam, over the centuries they have been dominated by many different rulers — among them the Mongol leader Genghis Khan and the imperial powers of China's Qing Dynasty. Their sparsely populated land of great deserts and high mountain ranges is hard to defend. People live in separate oasis towns, more loyal to their own oases than to any national state. Even so, the Uyghurs preserved their own language and culture. They lived as they had from the earliest time of the old Silk Road, managing their limited resources of land and water and continuing their rich tradition as expert craftsmen and traders.

Then, in 1949, the People's Republic of China discovered that the Uyghur homeland had an abundance of coal, oil, and gas reserves, in addition to gold and precious metals. The Han Chinese, with full support from the Communist regime, rapidly took over. By 2000, census figures showed that the number of Uyghurs in East Turkestan had shrunk from 90 percent of the population to less than half.

The Uyghurs protested the invasion of their homeland. The authorities responded with punishments. Though the Uyghurs practice a moderate form of Islam and are themselves wary of Muslim extremists, the authorities made an even greater effort to suppress them after the attack on the World Trade Center in 2001, with the excuse that all Uyghurs were potential terrorists. Uyghurs who take part in peaceful protests to protect their land and their distinct identity are sent to reeducation camps or prisons; many are tortured or executed. Such things as teaching religion to a minor and having a copy of the book *Dragon Fighter*, written by Rebiya Kadeer, the exiled leader of the Uyghur people, are considered criminal.

Unlike most of East Turkestan, the Hotan area where Mehrigul lives was left alone by the Chinese; it lies between the Taklamakan, one of the world's largest deserts to the north, and the Kunlun, one of the highest mountain ranges to the south. The area long remained a major stronghold of a pure Uyghur culture. In 2000 the population was 96.4 percent Uyghur. That has changed. The government is modernizing the city of Hotan; there is a new covered mall and supermarkets to attract tourists, although the ancient Sunday bazaar is of greater interest. There are discos and nightclubs. As the Han Chinese population in the area grows, land is being taken from the Uyghurs and their careful conservation of the water supply is being ignored. Uyghur teachers who do not speak Mandarin are being replaced; jobs created by the government are offered to the Han Chinese.

Memories of ancestors who have been one with their own land for centuries linger in the minds of the Uyghurs. The Uyghurs understand their bargain with the desert, the windblown sands from the Taklamakan that from time to time sting people's faces and bury their fragile oasis in a layer of sand. There is no escape from this timeless force of nature. The people cover their faces, shut their doors, yet the sand seeps through the weave of the cloth, the cracks in the walls. It passes. They return to their fields, their trades. As long as the spirit of their ancient culture remains true, they can endure.

But a storm has come to which there is no end. There has been no bargain made, no good understanding. The winds of change sweep over the Uyghurs in the name of progress. They struggle to make their voices heard.

A visitor traveling to Hotan and the countryside today would still see donkey carts, women wearing headscarves, men in their traditional four-cornered *dopa* caps, but Mehrigul's farm at the end of the poplar-lined lane might now belong to a family of Han Chinese.

ACKNOWLEDGMENTS

This book about the Uyghur people was made possible by the late Tom Wilson. Tom believed that travel to other countries was about meeting people and gaining an understanding of how they lived, rather than being an onlooker at established sites. Tom's World Craft Tours centered on visiting craftsmen and their families and watching them at work. Over the years he became a welcomed guest in many homes and shared this with a few who were privileged to travel with him, including me. Thank you, Tom, and thanks to Abdul, our Uyghur guide, who gave voice to the people we met in the countryside near the city of Hotan.

I wrote my novel with the help and support of my writers' group—Laurie Calkhoven, Bethany Hegedus, and Kekla Magoon—who were with me every Thursday from the first rough draft through to the final revision. Just showing up was important; you gave so much more.

I was lucky to have Ellen Howard, Liza Ketchum, the late Norma Fox Mazer, and Tim Wynne-Jones expect, and demand, the best of me while I earned my MFA degree from Vermont College of Fine Arts.

My deepest thanks to my agent, Marietta Zacker, who believed in me and my writing and found the perfect home for my novel. I am forever grateful to my editor, Dinah Stevenson, who cared about my story and helped to make every word in it the right one.

When I questioned my right to author a novel about a Uyghur girl living in Hotan, I sought the counsel of the Uyghur American Association in Washington, D.C. Henryk Szadziewski, manager of the Uyghur Human Rights Project, and Amy Reger, senior researcher, offered encouragement and guidance. They also introduced me to Mamatjan Juma, editor and international broadcaster at Radio Free Asia in Washington, D.C. He undertook the job of reading the manuscript and pointing out where the facts in my story veered too far from the truth. I am eternally grateful to him for keeping the story true to the spirit of the Uyghur people. Any errors or fictional liberties that remain, of course, are mine.

I wish to acknowledge Dr. Rachel Harris, ethnomusicologist at the University of London, for giving permission to use her English translations of the Uyghur songs.

And nothing would have been accomplished without the love and support of Bill.